A JOURNEY TO
ULTRADIMENSIONS

A JOURNEY TO ULTRADIMENSIONS

KOUROSH NAZIRI (CYRUS)

Ordering Information:
You may search this book in Amazon, Barnes & Nobles and other online retailers by searching using the ISBN below.

You may also visit the website www.cyrusn21century.com with discount.

ISBN (eBook): 978-1-952062-93-3
ISBN (Paperback): 978-1-952062-94-0

The US Review of Books

"'... good thing I have a sense of humor. If it was anyone else from my group, your arm socket would have ended up in there."'

At long last here is a science-fiction adventure story that couples the highs and lows of comedic romance with the far-reaching implications of drama told across multiple dimensions. A cycle of continuous space and an acceleration of multidimensional growth serves as the unusual backdrop to a familiar narrative. At its core, this tale seems akin to the mythical or lyrical folklore of our past. It resembles the kind of cataloged history, high drama, and linear conflict that would be told around a campus in every primal culture.

The story features Captain Houshmand, a great and brave man who is about to many his fiancée, Delaram. He is also world-weary and comically, has no tune to be the story's narrator. Instead, he makes his AI, Ryaneh, recount the tale. What follows is a space odyssey so fascinating that it could have populated a Homer voyage or a Flash Gordon serial.

Thus lies the great strength of this book. It goes into great depth about the logistics of time travel and the interconnected functions of endless dimensions. It consumes the reader's attention with its humor and colorful imagery while also demanding total concentration as it outlines an entire galaxy of varying elements. Everything from the details of a spaceship ready room to a different format of presenting comedy is all laid out by the author with total faith in the audience's ability to relate. It is a challenging and prodigiously engrossing piece of science fiction writing. From an AI with no social grace to an engineering staff that uses a universal language translator to communicate, one can't help but enjoy this richly detailed journey across space.

- Reviewed by: Robert Buccellato

Pacific Book Review

One of the most fascinating subjects that scientists and writers alike are always looking into is the concept of multiple dimensions, or even the multiverse. As H.P. Lovecraft once said, "Children will always be afraid of the dark, and men with minds sensitive to hereditary impulse will always tremble at the thought of the hidden and fathomless worlds of strange life which may pulsate in the gulfs beyond the stars, or press hideously upon our own globe in unholy dimensions which only the dead and the moonstruck can glimpse."

In author Cyrus's novel *A Journey To UltraDimension (Time of No Essence In This Ultra Dimensions)*, the author showcases a short story about a man named Captain Houshmand.

The author has crafted a very creative story with a unique approach to the narrative.

Told from the perspective of the protagonist after the battle has already happened, the Captain narrates the events of learning of Delaram's disappearance, traveling through multiple dimensions and facing untold peril. While a short read, the author conveys a lot of creative storytelling into a brief amount of time, and also infuses some fascinating scientific theories about dimensions which many readers will be invested in.

The story would be perfect for anyone who enjoys quick, enjoyable sci-fi reads. While I found the story highly engaging and fun, the one thing I will make note of that readers will notice is that the story does need both formatting and editing somewhat. The novel will at times switch back and forth between past and present tense, and yet the story still was impactful as it touches on the high points so many dedicated sci-fi fans look for in a story.

This was an interesting, fast-paced yet engaging science fiction read. Author Cyrus and his story *A Journey To UltraDimension (Time of No*

Essence In This Ultra Dimensions) is an exciting thrill-ride of a sci-fi adventure that you won't owant to miss, so be sure to check it out for yourselves today!

-Reviewed by: Anthony Avina

Portland Review

Journey to the UltraDimensions is a science fiction adventure story between Captain Houshmand and the Xinterrians and Meh-jazians. The story begins with Captain Houshmand's fiancée, Delaram, being kidnapped by the Xinterrian leader, Zieman Kahn. Captain Houshmand will need to rescue Delaram and save planet Earth from the Xinterra and Meh-jazians invasion. On his way back to Earth after he learned about the kidnapping, Houshmand ended up in a different dimension that resembled Earth. General Sherner, the leader of the UltraDimension station, explains to Houshmand why he is there. Houshmand, who possess special qualities, must right a wrong from the past. Houshmand returns back to Earth equipped with some great advice from General Sherner. An epic battle will ensue. Can Captain Houshmand save Delaram and Earth from an evil invasion?

The author obviously knows a lot about electronics and it is evident in the story. I like how feisty Delaram was, speaking incoherently when they beamed her out of the robot. Surprisingly, she then slaps Houshmand for taking so long to rescue her.

At times, the story felt as if I'm reading a summary of the story. Instead of letting the reader experience the events in the story, the author tells the reader directly what is happening. For instance, the author tells us something is funny instead of letting us experience the humor, which is counterproductive. Unfortunately, the book needs additional formatting and editing. The book reads like one long paragraph.

There's barely any quotation marks and proper spacing, so it made reading the story very difficult and harder to follow. Proper formatting would help organize and make reading the story easier. Overall, the story has a lot of promise, but it needs some work.

-Reviewed by Helen Vernier

San Francisco Review

He has a passion for concepts like ultra-dimensions.

Characters in this story include Captain Houshmand, his kidnapped fiancé Delarem, a robot, and a leader of the monsters named Zieman Khan, a chief engineer named Carolyn Sanchez, Lieutenant Chang, and others. The plot deals with ideas like an imminent attack on Earth, hidden bombs on Earth, and a love story. It covers many dimensions and references to some historical figures back in time. It's a multicultural story, as it includes references to the Punjabi language and features both male and female leads.

-Reviewed by Lynn Elizabeth Marlowe

Seattle Review

A Journey to UltraDimensions is a decidedly odd beast. Billed as a science fiction/adventure novel featuring romance and a touch of humor, it actually reads more like a treatment for a television series or as the preface or first story in a space opera collection. At under twenty pages in length, the story offers only a whistle-stop tour of the author's many interesting ideas, although the overall plot and some characters do show promise.

The backdrop to the story is a war raging between humanity and the diabolical Xinterrians. Fearful that humanity are preparing to deliver a knock-out blow to his planet, Zieman Khan, the leader of the Xinterr, hatches a plot to disrupt humanity's plan: he kidnaps Delaram, the beautiful fiancée of Earth hero Captain Houshmand. This prompts Houshmand, accompanied by his loyal crew and his robot sidekick Ryaneh, to venture into space in search of Delaram. Unfortunately, Houshmand is unaware of the existence of ultra-dimensions and of the powerful alliance that Zieman Khan has forged.

This brief outline will likely seem familiar to science fiction fans, and that's no bad thing. Intergalactic warfare, deadly rivalries, thwarted romance, and the coexistence of multiple dimensions are all interesting and popular aspects of the genre. The issue with *A Journey to UltraDimensions*, however, is one of execution rather than of concept. The story is simply far too short to do justice to the many ideas the author tries to pack in. For instance, the background to the war needs to be made clearer if readers are to really care about it.

The concept of ultra-dimensions could be the novel idea that differentiates this story/universe from the rest of the genre, but only if the author expands on it considerably. Captain Houshmand has the potential to be an interesting character, but again, more background detail and real-time action sequences are required to make readers care about him. Ryaneh seems to be the author's favorite character, and he's certainly the best developed of the book's cast, but most of the attempts to use him to add humor to the story fall rather flat. Less explanation of why the robot should be considered funny would help here. To use the dreaded phrase: show, don't tell. This is another issue that could be resolved by lengthening the story.

A Journey to UltraDimensions is based on an intriguing concept and packed with many potentially interesting ideas, but it doesn't quite work as an entertaining story in its current form.

-Reviewed by Erin Britton

Manhattan Book Review

I began this book with high hopes. I've been in love with science fiction since I was a kid, watching *Star Trek* and playing with blocks on commercial breaks. A book dealing with other dimensions (or, as this book calls them, ultradimensions) sounded very promising, especially when I read the author had a background in studying electronics. Surely such a combination could only lead to an intriguing look at dimensional travel.

They delve into the action, introducing subplots and complications, and have a vast array of memorable characters. While this book does have many characters, most are mentioned once, and their defining characteristic tends to be their nationality rather than any aspect of their personality. The action, too, is lacking. While there is a climactic battle just outside of Earth's atmosphere, most of the action is told to us rather than shown through the narration.

In theory, the most comedic moments come from Ryaneh, but most of those are physical comedy, which would translate much better to a TV show than to a book. The rest is made up of comments on the accents of various minor characters, a type of humor which is, at best, hit-or-miss.

By the end, the book reminded me of nothing so much as the episodic science fiction shows of the 1970s. It has action, characters who are larger than life, and a robotic sidekick who shows up only for comic relief or to make the protagonist look good. However, there is a reason those were TV shows rather than books...

-Reviewed by Jo Niederhoff

Major Russell the new administrator at Cahcashon space station comes to the conference room.

Major: Good morning. As you know I am the new administrator for this space station. My name is Commander Russell. I am responsible for management of this military, scientific and technological space station. I am from the United States, from California to be exact. You are the senior officers. I am proud to serve with such impressive officers. I am honored specially to meet captain Houshmand the hero of the battle against those monster Xinterrians.

At this point all of senior officers gave a hurrah and big hand to captain Houshmand and Major Russell.

Captain Houshmand gets up and shakes Russell's hand humbly: major, honor is all ours we have heard a great many things about your heroics.

Lieutenant Chang, the manager of security of the station: Gentlemen you two are the best that I have known. I am sure we will have a good working relation in here. After we heard your records of service

I am sure you are a more suitable administrator than the previous commander Al Hemar.

Russell interrupts: How do you figure all of your deductions.

Lieutenant Chang: I have never served under anyone making mistakes all the time like Al Hemar.

Ryaneh the captain's Robot shows a hologram of the joker subroutine: anybody is better than Hemar, especially you major.

Everybody in the conference room starts laughing at the joker. Houshmand blushes at the rudeness of the joker. He immediately shouts: joker off.

Joker in the hologram runs toward something that looks like an exit in holographic screen. Just like cartoons this Human comedian jumps in the air and starts swinging his feet in the air like a bicycle rider and drum like cartoon is heard while he is not moving. Then all of a sudden, a bullet like sound is heard from the robot, and joker zooms out.

Russel: I have never seen anything like this, what is this captain.

Houshmand: This is a gift from my fiancée "Dellarom". She thinks I am too serious, she is trying to remedy my seriousness. I would have gotten rid of this robot long time ago, if I did not care about my fiancée.

Capitan Houshmand stares at the calendar. Russell notices him.

Russel: captain, are you staring at the calendar?

Houshmand: OH I am sorry I got distracted for a moment.

Ohashi: are you missing your fiancée? We know you are getting married in two months.

Russell nods as a sign of understanding.

Houshmand: In my country we have a custom. If something good is happening to you, you will treat your friends with something. Houshmand says something to Ryaneh the robot.

Ryaneh: I will be right back.

Ryaneh comes back with a tray full of cups of Darjiling tea, and special Persian Danish called Koluche, and serves the senior officers. Officers like the treatment received.

Ohasi: Oh captain we really like your custom and refreshments. So in the behalf of officers I thank you. Ryaneh turns into joker subroutine immediately. Joker shows a hologram of the Joker with an oversized moustache while the mustache was going side to side.

Ryaneh: Don't touch my moustache" lieutenant Ohashi.

Houshmand: stop this insolence at once, Ryaneh.

Ohashi: Ryaneh did not insult me. The phrase "Don't touch my moustache" in Japanese language means: "You are welcome". What a proper answer Ryaneh.

The tickle bone was tickled on the whole audience, including captain Houshmand.

Russel: Guys thank you for welcoming me I am really enjoying myself.

Ryaneh: I usually come up with my own jokes. The other day I was watching an old movie. I got this humor from the movie.

After a while Russell announces: The meeting is adjourned.

On the way out Russell: Captain, can you tell me about the previous commander ie Al Hemar.

Captain: I don't usually gossip. But I am doing a report about Alhemar. I was ordered to provide such a report by the space commission. This report provides a review on all of the senior staff.

Russell: Give me the highlights of some seniors and the previous commander.

Houshmand: yes sir. Al Hemar was an odd ball. He often made wrong decisions. He almost caused us defeat to Xinterrians, by making wrong decisions. He commanded most of the fleet of Cahcashon station to go fight at Mentar at the other side of galaxy. He ordered me and a bunch of defenders to Kamin strategic location at the neutral zone. I had told him that the Xinterrians will attack earth at Kamin.

Russell: I know about your heroic maneuvers at Kamin, especially that you were short staffed for the enormous number of the enemy

Houshmand: yes sir, thank you. I know I am comparing apples and oranges, but in terms of decision making Hemar was the opposite of lieutenant Ohashi. When she makes a deduction or analysis, you can bet on it. Hemar's crown achievement was to prove me wrong in an argument. I told him that we should go to Kamin and going to Mentar was wrong. It was like chasing after wild goose, in my language like going after black chick peas. As you know there are no black chick peas nor it is fruitful to chase after wild goose. In response he paid some scientists to develop a hybrid of chick peas with black beans. AndIn a few months he will provide his product.

Russel: How back warded and arrogant of Hemar to jeopardize our military interests, just to prove his views. Thank you Captain. I will wait for your report tomorrow. We are all tired. I think I want to go to bed.

Houshmand: yes sir.

The next day, Houshmand brings his report to Russell.

Houshmand: good morning sir, while he takes a glance at the big clock in Russell's office. It was 11:45 in the morning.

Russell: Yeah Captain you made the report very quickly.

Russell was a quick read. He was able to finish the 5 page report in 2 minutes.

Russell: good job captain with all of the mistakes of Hemar, your commander officer, you managed to defeat the mighty Xinterians. I see, you have used the space commission's recommendations for tactical maneuvers. For example, Zeita the newest commissions tactical patterns. I also see that you have come up with a couple of your own patterns. These patterns are so delicate that I believe not anybody can understand the delicate points.

Houshmand: thank you sir.

Russell: for example this pattern Epsilon of yours, I like you to elaborate on it. How did you come up with it and why was that so determinant to defeat the Xinterrians.

Houshmand: well sir. I don't know how to say it so I just say it.

Russell: forget about formalities. You are ok with me.

Houshmand: The answer to all of your questions is one or two sentences. That is what I had found out about Xinterrians some time ago. I think Xinterrians IQ is about the size of my shoes. They have a hard time comprehending issues. They have a hard time applying their learning to experience. They do what somebody tells them to do. If there are any changes in battle scene, for not knowing any better, they will do whatever they have been doing. By changing something in the battle you can really gain a very big advantage.

Russell: so, what did you change and consequently what did you do?

Houshmand: I ordered my team to pretend that they have lost and run. Then Xinterrians would send a portion of their fleet to chase after us. Our team agreed to meet up at a location after they had scattered all over. Then we turn around and attack the Xinterrians. We repeated this strategy 2 or 3 times. This way we divided the Xinterrians to smaller groups. So, at the convergence point they would be surprised, confused and, lose. As you know because of mistakes and wrong strategies of Al Hemar a lot of our fleet were chasing so called goose at the other side of the galaxy.

Russell: Whatever happened to Alhemar's black chick peas? Has he finally achieved his goal to say whatever he says goes?

Houshmand: the space commission has relieved him of ranks and duty. But don't worry about him. He has a lot of rich supporters I am sure he would pursue another project after his chick peas. FYI: he has not fulfilled his project completely. He managed to make his chick peas a little darker.

Three weeks later alarms are sound due to a request by lieutenant Chang.

Russell shouts: Chang report. What is happening?

Chang: We have detected some neutrazine by our far range scanners. Seems like in a passenger-cargo ship, there are some Neutrazine and contraband materials hidden. Since we are close to Xinterrian's neutral zone, I presume they are heading for Xinterria. With earth's sanctions on Xinterria. This cargo can be a threat to earth.

Houshmand: The cargo ship is only 2 hours from us. I volunteer with my team and I go immediately to intercept.

Russell: My sentiments exactly.

Ryaneh at the operations terminal: It seems like, for intercepting a small cargo ship two fighter ships should be enough. Ohashi since the neutrazine seems to have military applications, I recommend more fighter ships.

Russell: Good call Ohashi.

Captain Houshmand and 3 more fighters depart one by one. Starting with captain Houshmand followed by his wingmen, the mission started.

Houshmand on COM 1 the main communications channel: public announcement for the team "we are dealing with a dangerous gang of bootleggers. My sensors picked up the insignia of the cargo ship. It is from Jorn cargo group. They are armed and dangerous. Expect what you don't expect.

Wing man and fighter ship 1: This is Lieutenant Rodriguez. Roger team leader."

Fighter 2: this is captain Chander. Roger team leader."

Fighter 3: this is captain Le Baron. Acknowledged.

After going a few miles Houshmand: We are entering Gaze Nebula, Which is mainly ammonium gas. Slow down a little bit as the friction, and heat will increase too much if you go faster than .01% warp, especially with that angle of entrance.

The wingmen acknowledged one by one, as they were within 50000 kilometers from the nebula. The wing men following captain Houshmand started to decelerate.

As fighters reaching for the outer borders of nebula, Captain: Team members, start accelerating toward warp speed. Note: this is a manned mission do not exceed 9g's of acceleration, or we might get heart attack or other problems. We are in an intercept course to Jorn cargo ship.

Rodriguez: fighter 1 roger.

Chander: fighter 2 roger.

Lebaron: fighter 3 roger.

In a few minutes the team arrived at vicinity of the interception point.

Houshmand: cargo ship Jorn do you read me.

Houshmand repeated the message 3 times.

Jorn cargo ship responds: This is Jorn cargo ship. We are hauling sick patients. Please let us be on the way. We are on the way to Venus memorial hospital on planet Velora, which is best treatment facility for Ebolom. Ebolom viruses can cause devastating pandemic. We need these patients admitted as soon as possible. They are suffering from highly contagious disease.

Captain Houshmand immediately realized that the destination is actually Xinterria. Velora planet is on the way to Xinterria. This way the cargo ship is trying to evade the fighters and not say they are on the way to Xinterria.

Houshmand at the bridge of his ship ie. Simorgh fighter ship: Ryaneh, mute the communications to Jorn cargo ship first. Give a message through beta channel to teammates. Send the message by Theita codes.This way I could keep communicating with Jorn without them finding out what I was planning or if I even know about Neutrozine in Jorn's cargo bay.

Houshmand: Ryaneh, unmute the communications with Jorn cargo ship. Cargoship jorn, you are hereby ordered by space commission's authorized agent that while you are in earth's territory, you will cooperate with us. You will discharge your phasors by short circuit and lower your shields.

Captain Rendman of cargo ship: as I said and I repeat we are in a hurry to get to Venus memorial hospital. Please let us go.

Houshmand: Rendman you lower your shield and short circuit the phasors immediately or else.

Rendman at Jorn cargo ship: ensign Bortar, Houshmand has found out about us. He is onto us. Our trick did not work. Immediately open fire on Houshmand's Simorgh ship.

Houshmand to Ryaneh the robot: Fortunately, I and the team have already raised our shield. What is the status of damages to the ship and the shield integrity?

Ryaneh: The Jorn phasers did not do any damages to the ship. Simorgh is the fastest ship in Cahcashon space base. With proper maneuvering and using shield, nothing else is expected.

Houshand immediately talks to team mates: Go to pattern zeita, so that we can evade the Jorn's further firing.

Rodriguez: team leader, Zeita pattern acknowledged.

 The other two wing men also acknowledged. All four ships followed the Zeita divergence pattern.

Captain Houshmand to wing men: As you all know, due to Neutrozine in cargo ship, firing at Jorn is like a suicide. On the other hand we could not let cargo ship Jorn's Rendman get away with hauling Neutrozine to Xinterrians.

Houshmand: This is captain Houshmand of earth's space commission. You will surrender or face the consequences.

Rendman: we will never surrender.

Captain Houshmand to wingmen: start to fire on Jorn's engine. Set phasors at the weakest setting. If we could prevent Jorn from moving the bootlegged nitrozine to Xinterians, we go on with the next phase of this offence against cargo ship Jorn.

Le Barron on Houshmand's wing: Unfortunately cargo ship, Jorn's engines did not get a serious damage when I fired at them. I am trying a new maneuver to get closer to the cargo ship. I will try a jolt of phasor on the Cargo ship's engine.

Le Baron after his maneuver: cargo ship Jorn's engine got a serious damage now.

Houshmand: I can see smoke coming out of the cargo ship. Good job Le Baron. The Jorn cargo ship's engines are disabled. Now Cargo ship captain cannot escape us. Pretty soon the cargo ship will enter the Segami planet and the atmosphere will halt the ship. It is my turn now. Here I go.

At Simorgh, captain Houshmand: Ryaneh, target the Jorn's weapon array. I will try to go near Jorn's weapons so you have near surgical accuracy hitting the weapon array. I will get within a few Kilometers of the bootlegger's ship. Counting down. We are 2 thousand Kilometers to the target. Keep the course. Do a bee flight pattern to avoid the enemy fire.

Ryaneh: general course set. Pattern Hornet bee for maneuvering chosen. Ready for your command to fire at the bootleggers. But sir it is getting hard to avoid the Jorn cargo ship's fire. I think the enemy is on to us.

Houshmand: Change course to the flank side of the enemy ship. Same pattern and course.

Ryaneh: The enemy fire continues, but it has been reduced. Increasing speed and wider flight domain has helped too.

Houshmand: 1,500 kilometers and closing. Keep on Ryaneh...... 1000 kilometers. 500 kilometers. Three hundred kilometers and closing.

Ryaneh: Our speed is increasing, faster than ever. We are getting too close captain.

Captain: set phasors as target. Ready.... Fire.

Ryaneh: weapon array suffered a direct hit captain. I see second set of smoke coming out of Jorn, the engine and the weapon array.

Captain Le Barron: Good shot captain. I see more smoke coming out of Jorn. They have to use thrusters to change course to planet Segami now.

At Jorn ship Lieutenant Reeper: The engine and weapon array are hit Captain Rendman. What are your orders?

Rendman: we have no choice but going toward the Segami planet. Set the most direct path to Segami. Due to Segami's atmosphere we will start to slow down. Hopefully we will lose the space commission's armed forces. Then we can land on the surface of the planet and start with repairs.

Reeper: I am not sure if we have enough momentum with little size and little gravity of the plane to clear Segami's atmosphere at the proper location. The gravity will pull us toward the mountain area.

Rodriguez: Captain Houshmand, Jorn will halt near the Segami's outer atmosphere. With the gravity pull and Jorn's thrusters they can land at Mountains area of the planet. Here is my estimate of the location of landing. May be Ryaneh can confirm our calculations, captain Houshmand.

Captain Rendman at the jorn cargo ship: I see gravity is pulling us in. we will use the thrusters to land. I see a mountain range and some boulders nearby. Everybody in the ship get ready to run toward the mountainous area. If we get to the mountains we will have a good strategic advantage over the commission's forces.

Reeper from the Jorn's crew: Men we have been pulled by Segami the past half of an hour. On my command run for the mountains. Make sure you all carry your weapons.

Captain Rendman of Jorn: Good Idea Reeper! Everybody run. You all try to stay with Reeper and me till we arrive at a suitable camping area near the mountains.

Captain Houshmand: All of my team listen up, from tremendous smoke from Jorn Cargo ship we know they have landed near mountain area. Everybody get ready, get in your gear. We might have to fight the bootleggers. Land within the jungle near the edge of the desert, leading to mountains. We must hide our ships near the jungles. We don't want our ships fall in the wrong hands.

Rodriguez: roger captain.

Le Barron: Roger and out.

Chander: roger Captain Houshmand.

Captain Chander: I know this kind of jungle-desert-mountain areas very well. If I may captain Houshmand, I will take the lead with you. I know my experience will prevent us from getting lost.

Houshmand: we all are familiar with hard trains, but perhaps you are the best here. Lead on Captain. Everybody is aware that these criminals are armed and extremely dangerous.

Boot legger, Lieutenant Reeper near the edge of the mountain area: Captain Rendman I was just looking at the competition through my binoculars. They are within a mile of us and catching up. I recommend that since the law enforcement is very close, we should hide behind the big boulders. We won't have time to go to mountains for a better place to hide for having a strategical advantage. This way we can't hide but we have a better covering for ourselves.

Bootlegger captain rend man: I agree this is the best idea and break we have had all day. Arrange it Reeper. Find us the best place for cover. The law enforcement is coming soon.

Reeper: captain, I suggest those large boulders. We can hide behind them and can shoot at the law enforcement easier. There is not anything for the law enforcement to cover behind, from the direction that they are coming from. Men let's go behind those boulders, take cover and hide.

Captain Houshmand: this is bad cover for us. The bootleggers might be hiding in mountain or behind the large Boulders. Either way we are at a disadvantage. Let's Wait here and figure out how we want to do this.

Chander: I agree. We will be ambushed at the skirt of mountains.

Houshmand: I have an idea. How about if first we take cover behind those smaller boulders. But we won't have a good cover. As a matter of fact, we can only take cover if we lie down. Sitting or getting up would be a suicide. But with my plan will cover us from the fire of the enemy. Let me explain' my plan is ....

Chander: I can easily say yes to this tactic.

Le Barron and Rodriguez together: eye captain.

Rendman at the criminals' camp: men, I think I will try to look around for reconnaissance.

When captain Houshmand arrives, just about to the smaller boulders, villains start firing.

Houshmand: cover behind the small boulders and lie down for cover.

Houshmand at the camp: Here is Rendman and group shooting at us. They have killed three of our security officers. They are still shooting at us. I will take care of this. Cover me.

While Houshmand is getting up and shouting: Rendman I am coming for you.

Houshmand to his group, while covering behind the small boulders: As planned, I will throw a few smoke grenades starting within a couple of yards of the criminals. Then the following grenades will start away from the criminals ie toward our own direction. This way smoke will blind the criminals and won't be able to accurately aim at us. As I said before, wait for a few second and on my command by hand signal, we will charge toward the enemy. Everybody stay as quiet as possible until we get passed the smokes, around a couple of yards before we get to enemy, and then follow my Que.

Obviously Houshmand and his team's movements were hidden behind the smoke. Houshmand signals with his hand saying wait 20 seconds, while shouting attack, to confuse the villains. Rendman mercenaries start shooting fiercely, but in the air without hitting Houshmand's team. After 20 seconds Houshmand gives the order by a hand signal. The fierce Houshmand and team rush toward Rendman's mercenaries, while at the 2 yard line ie. Smoke clearance line Houshmand shouts.

Houshmand: attack. Awwww

Everybody in Captain Houshmand team starting to scream at the top of their lungs while starting to shoot at the enemy: AWWWWW......

Rendman's men were really surprised from the sudden attack and the aw's of Houshmand's team. There was roar of lasers herd in the scene. After losing a lot of men, Rendman surrenders. After securing Rendman and his mercenaries, Houshmand points to two of his men.

Houshmand: you group of men take inventory of the cargo ship. The rest of you secure the passengers. Everybody be very careful. Especially with the Neutrazine. Create a protective field around the Neutrozine to be delivered to the space station.

TWO MONTH AFTER

HOUSHMAND TO RUSSELL: THERE has been almost two months since the Rendman's excitement. It is so quiet since then. I have a bad feeling, as if there are going to be a storm after this silence.

Russell in a humorous way: You are getting jittery for nothing. Tomorrow is your wedding day. You better be on your way towards earth any minute now. I am here we get by without you for a few days. Houshmand: May be you are right major, but still …. I better start packing.

While packing, the speaker nearby starts broadcasting: Captain Houshmand, please come to the Com Link room. Houshmand goes to the communications room thinking that his fiancée is calling him for tomorrow's wedding. Janice his mother-in-law appears on the screen while crying.

Captain Houshmand: what happened? Is everything all right?

Janice: Something happened to dellarom a few hours ago. A group of nasty Xinterrians came to her apartment. They injured her roommates.

Two police officers and 2 Xinterrians were killed on the shooting exchange. Dellaram has disappeared with no trace.

While she became excited and fearful the mother-in-law continued.

Janice: Captain, hurry back to earth. Maybe you can catch these savages. So far, the police have not been successful to find any trace of her. Some of the Xinterrian terrorists have been immediately apprehended by the police. But it seems some of the terrorists have escaped. The arrested Xinterrians denied everything and say that they don't know anything about this. The answer to "then what are you doing on earth" was: "we don't know."

Captain Houshmand: don't worry mother. I will find her. I will give you my word.

Houshmand: mother I am glad you seem a little more relaxed. I will find her even if I have to search Xinterria by a tooth comb. Farewell mother.

Captain Houshmand disconnects at the telecom room, and rushes toward Russell's office. After telling the commander what had happened. Russell continues.

Russell: This is the day before your matrimony. I am sorry for what has happened. Is there anything I can do to help?

Houshmand: I need the fastest medium size ship, simorgh ship, sir.

Russell: I will call lieutenant Ohashi right away. Go ahead to the fleet hold of the station.

Houshmand arrives at Ohashi's office with a request paper in his hand. He knew How Disciplined Ohashi was.

Houshmand: did the major call you?

Ohashi: I just finished my conversation with Russell. The space fighter simorgh is the fastest medium size fighter ship in my fleet. You can have it.

Houshmand jumps in simorgh in a hurry. He takes his navigator-helms man robot ie Ryaneh with him. He immediately gives a command to Ryaneh the robot.

Houshmand:Ryaneh, joker off. I don't feel like talking to a comedian right now. Are you ready for this mission?

Ryaneh: yes sir.

Houshmand: get us out of the station. We are heading for earth.

Ryaneh is a compact robot. It is able compress and decompress to different sizes depending on its function. Captain Houshmand gives another command to Ryaneh to compress its size to the smallest size at the helm.

Ryaneh: Transforming to smallest size… forgive me if I make some robotic sounds.

Ryaneh changes its size gradually, from human size to the size of an encyclopedia. First it compressed its feet and legs completely while sitting at the copilot chair. It then minimized its hands and arms to a size just to control the helms and navigation duties. Ryaneh then compressed its height to the minimum also. Ryaneh sets the course and flies out of the station.

Although Simorgh was capable to jump to warp in a second. Ryaneh knew that humans or biological organisms will not tolerate such huge acceleration at once. It knew at 100g's for example a human might turn to puree even to molecules. So, thinking of Captain Houshmand, it set the acceleration to 9g. This way the ship can get to warp speed. Now the Simorgh is set to go to earth. Captain

Houshmand was thinking deeply as what to do to find his fiancée. He thought may be to talk to people in the vicinity of his fiancée's apartment. But he thought that the police have done that already. He then thought that he had no choice. It certainly will do no harm to investigate things again. Even interrogate the captured Xinterrians again. Unfortunately, the police with red alert status did not find any alien flight out of earth. Continuing towards earth Houshmand receives a communication from earth's police that they detected a ship flying out of earth, heading, for the space station.

Houshmand: Captain Houshmand calling Russell.

Russel appears on the Monitor at Simorgh ie captain Houshmand's ship.

Russell: Hello Captain, what happened?

Houshmand: Major asks lieutenant Chang to investigate any ships arriving at the space station around the time of Dellarom being kidnapped.

Chang: Chang here. There was a suspicious character by the name of Edenman from the Mars settlements. He wanted to talk to you. But you were having a conversation with the major at the time. So, he went to your office to wait for you.

Houshmand: I did not see anybody in my office. Perhaps it was a coincidence. Captain Houshmand continues toward earth with warp 12, the maximum speed of simorgh ship. On the way to earth captain realizes a singularity in space appears dead ahead.

Captain: Ryaneh, reduce the speed to near halt. Seems like there is no room to maneuver around this black spot in space.

Ryaneh: I am decelerating by 9g that is about 90 meters per second per second. This is recommended by space commission as the maximum acceleration allowed for manned missions.

Captain: spare me the unnecessary information. I am well aware of the space commission's recommendations.

Ryaneh: captain even though I am giving the command to computers at helm, and try to decelerate, the gravity force of singularity is pulling us toward it.

Captain: turn on all thrusters and the front burner engine to the maximum settings.

Ryaneh: I am already doing that captain, but no effect.

Captain: Then don't fight it. Turn all of engines off. Let's see where it takes us.

Ryaneh: Yes sir.

The singularity point or the black spot kept simorgh space ship toward itself more and more. Then stars and a fighter ship appeared in the far distance. This matter showed by long range sensors by Ryaneh. Hailing message arrived by the fighter ship.

Fighter ship: Hello captain Houshmand. This is major Recjer. If you can hear me please put me on screen and respond.

Captain: Ryaneh put him on screen. It seems that, this man knows me. May be even he can guide us home.

Holographic Screen shows a human in the command center of a strange fighter.

Captain: major Recjer, it is nice to see you. But I have never seen you before. How do you know who I am?

Major Recjer: We know about you captain, although you don't know us. You are in Ultradimensions now. Look at Your time recorder. It shows the time at 5:00 o'clock. When you leave here it would exactly be 5:00 o'clock. What I am trying to say is that time is of no essence in the Ultradimensions. Know then you will not spend any time by visiting us.

Captain: I am confused. I have a lot of questions.

Major interrupts him: I know that. The only thing that I am allowed to say is, you are here to correct a wrong. Let me escort you to our base.

Major Recjer escorts the captain to a tall white building with 2 strange structures rising from the top floor in a planet that looks exactly like earth. The captain noticed earlier that before major showed up, it seemed that he is approaching the solar system and earth. Also, the time was stuck at 5:00 o'clock right after the captain reached the singularity, until the time he noticed major Recjer. Captain was amazed at the similarity of this planet, and their solar system with earth's. It was surprising to the captain how different the surface of this planet was from earth. After a while captain arrives at the Ultradimensions base. On that place the captain was welcomed with a distinguished looking man who introduced himself as General Sherner. The general pads the captain on the shoulder.

General Sherner: Welcome captain you are at the dimension 1 of the ultradimensions. As you know, time is of no essence, in Ultradimensions. You could check with your time recorder and see that the time is still 5:00 o'clock. I am the director of this facility. I am very shorthanded right now. So, I apologize that, the major will guide you to our main computer that is called Jombina. Jombina will answer all of your questions. The captain is led to a desk holding a holographic screen computer. The computer was as small as a book, but the screen was huge. Major offers a chair to the captain near Jombina the Ultradimensions computer.

Jombina: welcome captain, to Ultradimensions. I am Jombina, the main computer in this facility. Go ahead ask me all of your questions. I am ordered by the general to answer all of your questions. You have noticed that this planet is very similar to earth but the surrounding, the buildings and, the environment is different. We are in another realm. As you know there is a long battle between the evil and heavenly forces. In this dimension we fight the evil. The evil has the upper hand in this battle right now. We hope with your help and, other things that are about to happen, we will turn the table on the evil. At this point the evil has a winning hand on earth. If we lose your earth completely, we will have a hard time winning this war. You should know at this point that the leader of Xinterrians ie,. Zieman khan and the leader of a powerful race called Meh-jazzians are having an agreement signed. The leader of Meh-jazzians is called Zohtar khan. I am afraid that your situation might be bleak if this agreement is signed. But for all practical purposes this agreement is a done deal.

Captain interrupts Jombina, the computer at the ultradimension's base: Excuse me may I ask you a question that just is haunting me to ask?

Jombina: Go ahead ask me.

Tired Captain: This word Meh-jazzian means cyber in Persia. Does it mean that Meh-jazzians are preparing a cyber-attack on our planet?

Jombina: although Mehjazzians are great at sneaky cyber-attacks, this is not an issue. It so happened that the residents of this planet call themselves the Meh-jazzians. The enemies of earth have started some kind of sabotage around the earth. Meh-jazzians chose the Xinterrians as an ally, the two are very similar in appearance and mentality. They understand each other very well. I don't know how much the enemy has been successful in the sabotages. Suffices to say that if they succeed there would be a lot of casualties around the earth. The earth is in imminent danger. The Xinterrians have a technology to teleport a lot of hidden explosives all across a lot of vast areas on earth. The other very powerful enemy of earth, called the Meh-jazzians has a grudge against the earthlings over a planet Meina. Apparently, earthlings know this planet as their own, while the Meh-jazzians have had their eye on Meina for a long time. Currently the earth is unaware of these Meh-jazzians. If these two forces join together, they can easily conquer earth and there would be so much casualty that you couldn't imagine how many. When you pass the singularity point toward out of this dimension you will observe the time would be exactly at 5:00 o'clock. So, you realize that any time has not passed. I was told by General Sherner that you must change your course from earth to Cahcashon space base, soon as you clear the singularity point.

Captain Houshmand: what is my role in all of this?

Jombina: You will debrief Major Russell of all of these facts. You must prepare for a bloody battle.

Captain: Why am I chosen for this mission?

Jombina: general Sherner has chosen you because of your heroics in battle against the Xinnterrians. Only with a starship and a few fighter ships you managed to beat the Xinterrians. There is another reason also, which is even more important than the first reason. You believe in good, you are honest and, clean. You have not committed anything against morality and beliefs.

Captain interrupts Jombina: Oh! Something unexpected just came to my mind. Now I know why my fiancée was kidnapped. If anything has happened to me then earth would suspect Xinterrians and might have taken some actions against them, starting with an investigation that could lead to the Xinterrians and preparation for a major offensive. In this case the elaborate scheme of Xinterrians might have been discovered, and earth might have taken a preemptive attack against the Xinterrians. Especially, now that the known enemy ie. Xinterrians been defeated, earth is somewhat relaxed.

Jombina: now I know you measure up to your name. As I understand Houshmand means wise in your country. It means a wise and intelligent man.

Captain humbly smiles: Please don't let me interrupt you go ahead with your presentation.

Jombina: By now you know how evasive your enemies are. Mehjazzians are so strong military wise. Perhaps they are the most powerful military in galaxy. They could single handedly beat the earth in a war. But they want to join the Xinterrians to lower their casualty. Also, they want to increase their chances in winning this war.

Captain: why don't you people come in to help our earth?

Jombina: We are very strong. But it is better for you if we didn't interfere in this matter. You will gain more enemies than you will benefit with our help. Besides we cannot help you, it is forbidden to interfere in other dimension's affairs. However, we can help you in other ways. For example we can give you vital information, if it is authorized information.

Captain: Is there anything you can do to help us?

Jombina: I can't tell you what decisions you should make to win. I know you are an intelligent person. If you choose wise, there is a good chance for winning. I can also tell you that in this fight you have to have better shield against the weapons of the enemies. We have a super shield in our dimension. It can withstand many kinds of photon torpedo, phasers and rockets.

Captain: Are you giving us the techniques for the super shield?

Jombina: We are ordered by general Sherner to give you this shield. It takes some time to prepare and implement it, but it will be worthwhile. We will also install a sophisticated multidimensional communicator in your ship. If we need you or you need us, we can communicate.

Captain: who are these Mehjazzians? What do they look like? How advanced are they in technology?

Jombina: I have bad news for you captain. Meh-jazzians are more advanced in technology and warfare. They are mostly, conmen. The technology that they have is stolen or taken by force or by sneak attacks on the weaker planets. They have gained a lot of technology by sneak cyber-attacks.

Captain: how do they gain all of these technologies? What is their Modus Operandi?

Jombina: they find a planet with a weaker military by research. Then they attack the poor planet, with a lot of infrastructure and life casualties. The poor enemy would be glad to give whatever they have just to get the Meh-jazzians off their back, whether science or technology. Meh-jazzians are ruthless and stone hearted. First, they kill then ask questions. Even if they get what they want there is always more casualty afterward. I hope that you understand that if Xinterrian-Mehjazzian alliance succeeds against earth, there would be an immense casualty on earth beyond what you would think.

Captain: what do Mehjazzians look like? Better yet I want to know all information about them.

Jombina:I have some bad news for you captain. The meh-jazzians are so advanced in technology and warfare than all of the earth. Most of them are ConMen. The technology they have are either stolen or bought from other planets in galaxy. A lot of their technology is acquired by Cyber-attack and hacking other planets' Cyber info structure. They find some planet that is advanced in technology, then hire mercenaries if they have to so that, the possible war ahead will come to their favor. When the meh-jazzians attack, they won't take prisoners they kill anybody and all they can kill by some outrageous number. They are very destructive and cruel. They like genocide to a level that you cannot imagine. They destroy a lot of victim's infrastructure too. The damages and casualties are so high that their enemy is brought to its knees. At this point the victim planet will give anything to get Meh-jazzians off their back. That is the point that Meh-jazzians will ask for all the technology and science the victim has. A lot of their technology is gained this way. Now the Mehjazzy's are at a point that they are the most advanced in science, technology and warfare in the galaxy. As you have guessed they are on evil side of forces. Besides enjoying killing and massacre the meh-jazzians are after the mark's technology and science. Unfortunately, the Xinterrians are after something else. I believe that you know Xinterrians very well. Zieman wants to enslave the entire planet. As you know these Xinterrians and Mehjazzians are the worst enemies that earth has ever had. If you and allied forces of Earth succeed to beat them in the future war, you will save the earth from a major catastrophe.

Captain: is there an advantage for you if we win?

Jombina: The advantage for us ie. The heavenly forces, is that we will turn the table around on evil. Currently the evil has the upper hand compare to us Ultradimensians.

Captain: What do Mehjazzians look like?

Jombina: They are somewhat humanoids. They have a pair of legs and feet, and a pair of hands and arms. Of course, they have an extra-long tail in their backs. In average they have five pairs of eyes and ears. As a general rule they are not artisans. They don't care about arts generally. Simply because of some audio-biological characteristic, whenever they hear an outstanding music they start to grow more ears, that shows they are moved by the music. They are very mean and unintellectual. Mehjazzians usually don't know what they have. They just have decided to fight and gain more. But they don't know how to maneuver around science and technology. Whatever they learn from the war victim or if someone teaches them, is all they know. If the situation changes, the jazzies are not competent enough to deal with the new situation. This would be an advantage for the earth.

Captain: you mean chance, situation, or strategy or whatever is the only hope that we have. Then we only have a praying chance in this war if we are wise?

Jombina: Yes you got it captain. They have no thinking process as a general rule.

Captain: With the descriptions you gave me about how strong the enemy is, with your information now we have a praying chance in this war ahead. For your information, Xinterrians are very much like that. I used the same techniques to beat Zieman Khan, the leader of Xinterrs.

Jombina: You can imagine these two enemies of earth are in love with each other since they are so much alike. Captain, what can you tell me about Xinterrs? The enemies both have long tails. But what can you tell me. I need to put you more information in my databanks.

Captain: Xinterians have one pair of eyes and one pair of ears. Their eyes are so big and weak. Xinterrs are slow minded. Perhaps they are semi blind. They have small ears. Perhaps in a funny way that is why, that they don't listen to reason. They used to have a strong military

Jombina interrupts: I know about your heroic fight with Xinterrians. You single handedly in a starship with a dozen fighter ships defeated the mighty military of Xinterrians. Captain that is another reason you are selected by general Sherner. You are indeed a military genius, and you are very intelligent.

Captain: I remember when I was debriefing Major Russell, a sore friend of mine commented about that "

"Yeah their IQ is the same size as my shoes. Perhaps that is why the captain was able to easily defeat them". It was so funny that the whole conference room started to laugh. A few security officers after initiation by Major Russell started to calm down the audience. Major Russell told the funny man, ie. Lieutenant Devoyst "perhaps it is time our funny man to apologize to the audience."

Lieutenant Devoyst says: "I apologize first of all. But you know, me and the captain are good friends. I didn't have any intention to insult the captain or the audience. "

Captain Houshmand: Russell said "Lieutenant Chang, please using a few security officers escort the lieutenant Devoyst to the exit.'

Captain Houshmand gets specifications of super shield from Major Recjer. The crew of Ultradimensions had already installed the intradimensional communications for captain Houshmand. It was almost time to go toward the Cahcashon space base. The captain says fair well to general Sherner and The major. So, the captain starts walking toward the ship along with his robot Ryaneh.

Captain: Ryaneh, you are again in charge of helms and navigation. Fire-up the engines.

Ryaneh starts the engines and turns on a lot of buttons on the ship. Lights start at the helms and navigational guidance system, confirming that the ship is getting ready.

Ryaneh: Everything is ready sir. We are ready to go.

Captain: Set course toward the singularity point. Now is time to move the ship out of here. Remember this is a manned ship so don't go beyond 9 g's of acceleration.

Ryaneh: Yes sir. If it was only me, I would jump to warp 12 at once. I know human biology's molecular bonding cannot tolerate even 100 g's without turning to as platter. Much less the accelerations like 30 millions of meter per second per second, ie. Jumping to warp in one second. The ship gets far from the earth of Ultradimension then out of their solar system. The singularity point gets close.

Captain: put the view of singularity point in the screen with maximum enlargement.

The singularity point shows on the Holographic screen. The ship is accelerating toward the point. After a while the ship is within one hundred thousand kilometers of the point.

Captain: Embrace yourself, Ryaneh. We are expecting turbulence, like the time we entered the singularity point last time. What time do the internal clocks show?

Ryaneh: The clocks are all synchronized at 5:00 o'clock sir. I will note the clocks at the exact time of exit out of the singularity point.

Captain: set course for the solar system. We want to stop at the Cahcashon space base.

Ryaneh: Done sir. The navigational guidance system is programmed. I will control the helm to Cahcashon.

THE ENEMIES CONTACT
CAPTAIN HOUSHMAND

ON THE WAY TO Cahcashon space base, a hailing message interrupts Ryaneh. A strange ship is approaching. Ryaneh has never seen such a strange huge ship.

Ryaneh: A huge unknown space ship up ahead is hailing us captain. What should I do?

Captain: Hail the unknown ship. Don't be concerned too much. If a ship this big wanted to destroy us they would have done that by now.

Ryaneh: This is the Simorgh space ship of earth, please identify yourself.

The unknown ship is helmed by Zohtar Khan the leader of the Meh-jazzians.

Zohtar khan: This is Tellian space ship of the Mehjazzia. Can I have a word with the captain?

Captain with an apprehensive face: This is captain Houshmand of the Cahcashon space base. Who do I have the pleasure of speakingwith? Ryaneh, put the ship on the holographic screen.

Zohtar khan: this is Zohtar khan of mehjazzia. I am companied by Zieman Khan of Xinterria. You should know that Xinterria and Meh-jazzia just became allies. We are here as a friend talking to you.

Captain was shocked and surprised. He asked himself what they want with him. He was also thinking how Zieman khan that he had defeated can come in peace and talk so friendly, especially, after what he had heard about ruthless Zohtarkhan. They are asking for a friendly discussion? He immediately realized that, this whole communication is a trick. So, he gathered himself and responded.

Captain: Go ahead how can I help?

Zieman khan was eating a very big bowl of cereal while Zohtar Khan started with a bossy attitude.

Zohtar khan: Hello captain, my name is Zohtar khan I lead the planet Meh-jazzia in far corner of this sector. I have a very good sense of humor too. So, let me tell you a puzzle.

Houshmand: go ahead.

While chuckling, zohtar khan of Meh-Jazzia: What kind of berries grows everywhere?

Captainwith a puzzled face: Please tell me.

Zohtar immediately started to laugh but tried to keep a straight face.

Zohtar: Bribery!

Zohtar became serious all of a sudden, with an attitude and posture, to show who the boss is.

Zohtar shouts while pointing at the captain: Hey, I like to get serious at this time. Listen I want to make an offer. I don't know how much you know about us Meh-jazzians. We are very powerful. Some people say we are the strongest planet in this galaxy. The attack against earth is imminent. You don't stand a chance. A lot of your friends would be killed. A lot of destructions are about to happen to your home planet.

Captain interrupted: Is that a peace offering?

Zohtar: I have a soft spot for bravery. I admire you for your bravery.

At this point Zieman khan Shook his tail a little and frowned. He was guessing that his stronger ally was probably referring to captain's brave fight with Zieman khan of Xinterria.

Zohtar khan: I will make a deal with you captain. We spare you and your family and friends, but all you have to do is to work for us. We really need information about earth's military weak points. We need real Intel. The reason is that I don't like lengthy wars, this way I can end the war quickly. In exchange I will be more merciful toward earth. I am very generous too. With this kind of money offering youcan stablish a very comfortable life for yourself. You can go anywhere after stablishing our deal.

Captain was not surprised.He learned in Ultradimensions that Zohtar khan is tricky, powerful, merciless and a con. He decided not to provoke Zohtar khan. Being alone in the middle of nowhere reassured his decision. But he knew the Khans were trying to fool him. Captain decided he won't get angry at khans.

Captain: zieman khan, you must be in love with cereals. I see a lot of empty boxes.

Cartoonamic subroutine ie Joker interrupts: Zieman khan that makes you a cereal (serial) killer.

Joker after his humor started to make his special funny laughs.

Captain: Mr. Khan I apologize for Ryaneh's rude behavior.

Then the captain makes a command to Ryaneh. "Joker off "

Joker: Uh oh I better go.

Just like cartoons the joker person jumps up, swings its legs and calf like driving a bicycle, in the meantime cartoon drums beat. Of course, at first, he does not move. Then a bullet or jet sound is heard. The joker starts running in a funny cartoons' way and gradually he disappears.

Zieman in a serious tone: Ok captain I heard your apology. Don't be a fool captain. I know you are in love with your fiancée. Don't you want to have a rich and happy life with your fiancée? Just cooperate with us, work for us and you will see prosperity and safety for yourself, and loved ones.

The joker was upset about Khans's innuendo about loyalty of captain to earth alliance. So, joker appears on Ryaneh's holographic screen.

Joker: You eat cereal so fast. Is it a mouth or vacuum cleaner? I am out of here.

Ryaneh then ends communications with the Aliens. The captain saw that he is no match for joker's mouth, and its insult to aliens might prove to be very dangerous. So, the captain orders Ryaneh to go with the maximum speed and acceleration possible. As ordered before by the captain, Robot sets the course toward the space station. Now the captain is assured and confirmed about the attack from two sources. First the Computer at the Ultradimensions, and now the Khans confirmed it again. He also knew this war would be the most devastating and fatal wars that the earth has ever had, if the enemy had a spy from earth on their side. He loved his fiancée with all of his heart, but he would never betray the earth and his friends. Besides, the captain knew that these enemies cannot be trusted. They will use him and then after the enemy achieved their goal. After very heavy destruction and casualty on earth the conscious alone will give him an aggravating death. On top of that Zieman Khan, because of the previous defeat will always hate him. Even if Zieman khan achieves victory now after the last defeat he will do anything to sting the captain again and again. The captain continues the road to the station and in a couple of hours reaches the destination.

Captain: Ryaneh, go to cargo hold and prepare a travel manifest for lieutenant Ohashi. Make sure everything is clean for her inspection. I will meet you in Commander Russell's conference room.

<hr />

MEANWHILE AT THE STATION

AFTER A LONG JOURNEY, from Ultradimensions to the space station captain Houshmand, very tired arrives at the space station. He decides walking will do him good. So, he starts walking toward Major's office. Cahcashon is a military, science and technology post with a lot of officers and experts in defense and technology.

Everybody in the station was enthusiastic to find out what had happened to the captain. The whole station was in chaos. Since the news of the war had arrived to station. Captain after talks with the khans had communicated the whole story to Russell.

The major had warned all of the staff, of the imminent war of the two Khans with earth. All of the staff of the space station, including electronic, mechanical, and structural, technicians, was working double time.

Captain informing everybody in station: I have had an adventure and never seen before journey. Our priority is the eminent planetary wars. We have an extremely important mission ahead of us to protect the love ones. Please take your minds off of my journey and do the best you can. I am sure with your expertise and dedications we will win the war.

Unknown cadet: We are certain we will win, especially with you on our side. We all know how you singlehandedly defeated the whole Xinterrian army.

The whole staff started to clap their hands for captain Houshmand.

Joker: My captain defeated the ridiculous Geginterrians I am sure with his help and Major Russell and all of you heroes we will beat jazjazians too.

Sanchez to Ohashi: this robot again is making fun of the names of the enemy. The enemy is too strong. Making fun of the enemy will get us nowhere.

Ohashi to Sanchez: Do you see everybody's high morality, and joy. They are ready to fight. You see confidence and no fear in faces. Do you want more?

Knowing how everybody respected Ohashi's opinions and deductions, Sanchez sighs in relief strongly, a symbol of less nervousness.

Lieutenant Sanchez in a less panicky voice: I need the electronic technicians at the Andromeda star ship on the double. Marques and Akbar go to Tusee starship.

Sanchez sent all electronic technicians to different ships to do the necessary repairs and do a level four diagnostics on each ship. She was pointing the technicians and where they are assigned to go. You could see a maestro leading her orchestra to the notes. You could hear music like any maestro conducting an orchestra so; you would hear scanners and diagnostics devices lead by Sanchez performed by technicians.

Sanchez: Ladies and gentlemen the electronics must be in ship shape. After repairs do a level 4 diagnostics at each element and circuit to make sure our fighters won't have major electronic problems. Mechanical and structural technicians do an Infrared diagnostics. Look for cracks and Imperfections. Also do a smoke-laser test for deep cracks and holes in engine and ships' outer structures. Don't hurry. Take your time and do one thing at a time. The scanners and electronic diagnostic devices were playing like a symphony.

Captain Houshmad: Major Russell, may we speak privately?

Russell: Sure let's go in my office. Must be important it seems.

Houshmand: I have all specifications of a super shield from ultra-dimensions. This shield will make us more resistant against an enemy that outnumbers us. I like all of our ships be equipped with the super shield.

Russell: I agree. Let's inform Ohashi and Sanchez too. But captain I know you have a very valuable experience with Xinterrians. I thought you may be able to inform the pilots what to expect.

Houshmand in a taunting manner to the enemies: Yes major, I might be able to say some things. I even have some maneuvers prepared to fit for the high IQ of our Xinterrian friends.

Major: From what you quoted me from Ultradimentions, Meh-jazians have the same high level of IQ. If you add up their IQs it almost reaches my shoe size.

Both commander and captain had a good laugh. Commander suggested to have a meeting in conference room to discuss captain's maneuvers with senior staff. He thought that Sanchez and Ohashi also must be informed about the super shield and its complications.

He added that senior ship captains and above must be consulted on these issues.

Russell: We need to inform all earth allies of many things. One issue is the super shield. We also might inform our allies of your accomplishments with the Xinterrians. And the fact that you have a special strategy for this war.

Houshmand: I agree with you sir, that would cushion against our defense confronting an alliance that outnumber us greatly.

Russell: I am going to call for a meeting in 5 minutes be there.

In five minutes, all of the senior staff was called to conference room. Announcement called for all of the captains of ships and their senior next level of captains. You could hear officers and staff talking.

One officer was asking the other one: What could major be talking about? Will he say that the enemy is more advanced in warfare? Or how the enemy out number us?

Second officer: Let's not forget that we have Major Russell and captain Houshmand plus the best of the fleet. Captain Houshmand can beat Xinterrians with his hands tied on his back. Major Russell is an expert in galactical warfare.

First officer with passion and anger: Do you know Mehjazzians? They outnumber us and are more advanced technologically. That monster Zohtar kaka! might order to kill mercilessly. We are talking about casualties on earth beyond anything in history of mankind. I think we are a bunch of preys going for slaughter.

At this point heads turned toward the first officer. You could hear "yeah I agree ". with more officers being pessimistic more and more.

Second Officer: First of all we have super shield installed in our ships. I hear that captain Houshmand brought it with him from Ultradimentions. I saw Sanchez and technicians were installing ours for our ship. I was writing a letter for my family. I sat in my room when I heard the technicians. They explained that is our new defense against the enemy. It can defend against all of weapons known in the federation. This is game changer. There is always a chance in any game. But … I think you are underestimating us. The officers went to conference room. Everybody was enthusiastic to hear Russell. The officers wondering if Russell was giving them boring Pep talk and idle chatter or he had something to say.

Russell: Ladies and gentlemen can I have you attention please?

People had lost their confidence they ignored the major and kept talking to each other. You could see fear in everybody's face. Lieutenant Chang started whistling. Chang's officers started to ask people to calm down and be quiet and listen. Security officers of Chang were asking people to first listen and if they had questions they could ask later. So, everybody got quiet and When Russell started to ask for the attention of the audience. The audience started to listen.

Russell: Ladies and gentlemen, my dear officers I know you that you all know what kind of brut and heartless the enemies are. But captain Houshmand, my dear friend has brought us super shield which would be resistant to most kinds of torpedo, phasers and even most kinds of Photon torpedo. I count on all of you to stun us with your performance. I have my friend captain Houshmand to fill you in with the strategies and Intel. He has made up a couple of maneuvers that he believes will give us an advantage in this battle. I have informed even the space commission's command center to submit this information to the proper staff.

Captain arrived at the podium. You could feel that moods were changing. People could not resist Hoorahs and clap of hands for him. The captain started his speech and his Intel. Among the Intel he mentioned how slow and shallow minded the enemies are. He mentioned major's joke about the enemy's IQ, which caused the audience a lot of comfort and calmness. The captain continued with his strategies ie Houshmand strategies number one, two and three. Everybody was amazed at the creative powers of the captain. At this point Admiral Kaisen from space commission arrived. One of the officers cried, top brass coming. His name is admiral Kaisen. He is the senior strategist of the space commission. After a little talk with Major Russell, the admiral asked for captain Houshmand.

Admiral: Captain you might know that I am senior strategy officer on the space commission. The commission expedited me to ask you to debrief me on your journey to this Ultradimensions.

Captain: May I have your permission to sit admiral?

Admiral: please sit down captain. I know you must be exhausted after a long journey.

Captain sat down and asked for a favor. He asked for his robot Ryaneh. I have logged the journey in the robot he will start the debriefing and I add things as we go along. Admiral agreed. He saw extreme fatigue on Houshmand's face. Admiral took one look and said go ahead. Ryaneh appeared in compressed mode. It looked the size of an encyclopedia. When Ryaneh arrived in major's office and got the order to debrief the admiral, the robot started to decompress. It became as large as an average human. Its robotic arms and legs began to come out.

Ryaneh: My captain was to marry his fiancée, after victory against the Xinterrians. A day before the matrimony, Xinterrians came and kidnapped His fiancée Dellarom. I have a simulation of the Xinterrians kidnaping Dellarom.

The Holographic screen came out showing how the Xinterrians acted. Ten Xinterrian commandos sneaked to earth near Dellaroms apartment. They blew the entrance door and proceeded to the security guard. They shot and killed the security guard. They ran toward the elevator. They arrived at Dellarom's floor. They exploded her apartment door, started to shoot her roommates. All of the roommates are in the central hospital, with critical condition. A police patrol arrives by the exploded entrance door. Calls for back up for an armed attack by aliens. By the time the backup arrived, the aliens would be gone. So, the police started to shoot at the Xinterrians. Five Xinterrians were killed before the Xinterrians kill the two police officers. The Xinterrians escaped while kidnapping Dellarom.

Ryaneh: After captain was informed of kidnapping of his fiancée, he proceeded to go to earth perhaps he could start his own investigation about the incident. On the way to earth, our ship started to accelerate toward a singular spot in space.

Ryaneh proceeded to inform the admiral the highlight of the journey. Ryaneh told the admiral how the defeated leader of Xinterrians swore in front of his associates to become even with captain Houshmand.

After his defeat Zieman Khan of Xinterria, was forced to surrender under Earth's terms and conditions. One of the worst sanctions was enforced on Xinterria. Zieman khan could not fit in his skin till he gets even with the captain. At this moment lieutenant Sanchez knocks at the door and interrupts the conversation in the Major's office.

Sanchez: I Beg admiral's pardon. I have detected a signal initiating from this room. This signal is in a coded form and I have never seen anything like it.

Chang: Although it might be a legitimate signal but we can't risk it. Admiral, I recommend that we evacuate this deck sir.

Admiral: OK do it. I think we are done with debriefing captain. Do you have anything to add?

Captain: the most relevant outcome of the journey has been said here. I can say that I have nothing more to add sir. You already know my suggestions of defense strategies for this battle sir.

Admiral: then major, prepare for evacuation of this part of the station. I think I am done here. I would adjourn now to earth to debrief the space commission.

Sanchez: Roland, and Akbar, sweep the vicinity of the commander's room to find the source of the signal.

After a long search the team of Sanchez determined that the message was coming from the robot.

Russell: may be a bomb or spyware was installed in the robot by the aliens. Good thing that we evacuated this section. A broadcast was announced for everybody in the station to avoid this section.

Houshmand: major, there is nothing to worry about. Except this space station the robot has been my companion the whole time. Also, I have diagnosed the robot twice before allowing it to enter the station. But major, although this robot is made with the most sophisticated technology, for some reason it still has some the 20th century software in it, the communications module also might have it.

Russell rushes to communications link room to call his old friend, who used to be the senior engineer at the space station, before retiring. Russell thought that may be Jack Jones the previous senior engineer knows how to clear this dilemma. After some small talk Russell asks Jones how the retirement treats him.

Russell: a very strange coded message came from the robot. Sanchez my chief engineer and the engineering staff can't figure out what it is.

Do you have the time to come here to give us some assistance, Jones? By the way you live close by, why don't you come by quickly.

Jones: I will be there in an hour.

In one hour Jones arrives at the station. A white mustache and a goaty beard and white hair gave Jones some distinguish. In a working jump suit, with a couple of very fine tip screw drivers in his front pocket. A slim, robust look and Jones' agility was also noticeable. Jones was completely debriefed about most relevant facts about the situation. Jones then took the recorded message to the engineering lab, where Sanchez gave him a big bench to work at. After one hour Jones comes back with the results of his analysis.

Jones: This is an old communications coding. It repeats a message on and on. The message says basically "I am a ROM my name is DELLA". "I am burning. Please take me out". As you know ROM is vastly used in computers. ROM means Read Only Memory chip. Apparently, this chip is malfunctioning. The chip apparently has a self-diagnosis system. The diagnosis revealed to the chip that it is burning out. I wouldn't worry major. Just replace the chip. And the problem will be solved.

Russell calling Houshmand on the communicator: Captain Houshmand please come to my office.

Even Jones knew about the captain's reputation both as a hero and how precise he wants to do things. So, when the captain arrives in Russell's office, Jones starts to talk.

Jones: In my opinion this is a burned down chip. I can easily replace it for you captain. It would be my pleasure. I know how you are interested in details and accuracy. So, I will read you the entire message as it was sent.

Captain: go ahead Jones. But I want every detail.

Jones: This is my interpretation captain. There is a ROM chip called DELLA that is malfunctioning. You need to replace it.

Houshmand with an exited voice: Jones, I beg you could you repeat the name of chip?

Jones: It is a Rom unit called DELLA.

Houshmand shouting, and breaking in tears: Dellarom is my fiancée. What is she doing inside the robot? How can we take her out and save her life?

Jones: please give me a couple of hours I will think of something.

Russell: Jones, get together with Sanchez, consult together to see what you can do about this. Houshmand, I remember when you went to comm-room to talk to your mother-in-law, Edenman from Mars was here. He wanted a technician to look at some big electronics equipment. He must have sneaked her here and at the proper moment teleported her into your robot.

Captain: Edenman, Huhh! What an evil genius. My fiancée has been Right under my nose all of this time! I never knew that Martians, especially this Edenman hated me so much.

Russell: from what I hear Martians who are a few thousand of earthlings, settling mars have had some problems with earth. I didn't know they would go this far. Captain, don't take this personally. Edenman is a rascal adventurist, who will sell his mother and father, even his own child to get money and power. I am not sure that all of settlers of mars feel like Edenman. Houshmand, we will participate in an urgent conference along with the high senior officers to see how to save your fiancée's life.

Ryaneh beside the navigational and technical expertise had joker subroutine for entertainment. This subroutine was given to captain by his fiancée, Dellarom. While the captain was in his corner deep into his thoughts and thoughts about Dellerom, joker appears. Ryaneh decides to entertain the captain. Joker subroutine is activated. Joker decides to do one of the cartoonamics for captain. These cartoons like moves were recorded in Joker subroutine. A lot of episodes were recorded. Anytime the subroutine was called, a scenario is played, but Ryaneh would change the scenario for each time to fit the appropriate thing that was going on at the moment. Of course, cartoon sound effect was also accompanied with cartoonamics. Things like a jet whistle or fast beat drums etc. A famous funny comedian was hired to record all possible scenarios that the director of cartoonamics could think of. The comedian is really a very agile stuntman-gymnast to make these incredible moves possible. Of course the comedian was attached to a few ropes so that when he plummets, the actor is not really hurt. These ropes with the aid of cinematic tricks were invisible. So, the joker appears to entertain the captain. Joker in a cartoonamics scenario goes near a well and says I am in love with my fiancée and falling in love. I want to save her. Joker walks toward the well and does not see the hole in the ground. Then he falls in the well. Just to prevent falling, the joker then start moving his legs as if he is doing bicycle treading in a body of water. The joker is held in the air while he is doing water tread drums and funny cartoon sounds are heard in the back ground. Then the Joker says oh wow! Then he plummets toward the end of deep well. When he hits the ground, he only says ouch! And his teeth fall out. Then he magically gets a balloon and ascends toward the surface of earth. When he lands on surface. He greens and miraculously he has all of his teeth. All of these are funny attributes of cartoons children see on TV. But the difference is in here a real live person does all of this. However, having some ropes attached to the stuntman helps a lot. Let's get back to our story.

Houshmand in his ever serious tone: Ryaneh, I know you have good intentions. But you found a fine time to joke when a man is down and deep in his thoughts you know!

Ryaneh: Perhaps this is a little insensitive captain. You said it yourself that I had no bad intentions. At any event I really apologize, captain.

Before the captain had time to respond to his robot, a message from the Major is broadcasted all over the station. All senior technical staff and senior officers please report to the conference room in five minutes. Everybody called to conference starts running toward the conference room. Russell starts to debrief the senior staff as to what has happened with Dellarom and the robot.

Russell: officers, how can we take Dellarom back in good health? I want anybody who has an opinion to state his strategy. The retired senior engineer, Jones and current senior engineer Sanchez had thought about this matter before together.

Lieutenant Ohashi-chang had thought this together too.

Chang: we somewhat believe that the robot has to be dismantled. Then take the chip out and may be with adjusting the graphic enlargement technology, the lady will grow to her normal size. Of course lieutenant Ohashi is not very much persuaded with this procedure. We have developed a respect for Ohashi's deductions. Maybe, I want to say that, this is not a good idea.

Ohashi: I think lieutenant Chang is underestimating his talents. I liked this technology at first. But how do we know when to quit the enlargement? This is only one of the problems. Later on I found more problems, so I can't agree.

This was not approved as a viable option. There were several other options that were not agreed upon.

Jones: How about the teleporting technology. We use wideband energy concentrated in a fine beam of laser. We use teleporting to further enhance the lady. Sanchez and I have figured out the technical and mathematical parameters between us. This was accepted in the room with almost all of the votes from the audience in conference room. With confirmation of major Russell, and captain Houshmand this procedure was approved. It was broadcasted all over the station that a proper algorithm was chosen for saving Dellarom. And the whole procedure would be broadcasted on monitors for everyone in station. The staff cheered for Dellarom and Houshmand all over the station.

At the teleport room, all of the necessary staff is gathered. The staff is ready to start the operation with a command from Russell to proceed. All of the staff in the base was keeping an eye on monitors to see what was happening at the teleport room.

Houshmand: Ryaneh, let's go to the teleport room. Maybe we can save my fiancée.

Houshmand and the robot move toward the teleport room.

Jones: Ryaneh, go on top of the platform.

Houshmand: do anything Jones asks you to do.

The robot goes on top of the platform. He uses the ramp on the side of the platform to get to the top. Technicians use a device to concentrate the laser to a fine beam of laser. Jones and Sanchez both nod, indicating to the technicians to start the operation. A fine beam of laser is emitted to the side of Ryaneh. This side is the side that holds Dellarom.

Jones shouts: energize.

A heavy laser pulse is heard all over the teleport room. Then the fine beam is heard again when a second pulse of laser emitted at the platform next to Rayaneh. At first a hollow image of Dellarom appeared.

Sanchez: enhance this image with more energy amplitude and more bandwidth.

Jones nodded in agreement: major, is this platform enhanced to tolerate high energy bands.

Russell: yes Jones, it is made with special alloy Igraxium from mars. This alloy is stable and toughest alloy possible for this use.

Dellarom's image became richer and richer till it was a healthy looking human being. It was Dellarom. Naturally, everybody in station started to cheer. When Dellarom appeared, she had a tight sport jumpsuit. This appearance was exactly the same as when she was kidnapped. Dellarom was dazed and confused looking. As if she was in another world. She was staring at a blank space, ignoring his open armed fiancée and all of the cheering audience in the room.

Houshmand: Dellarom, are you alright?

Dellarom Ignoring Her fiancée turned her head around while she was uttering a strange language.

Dellarom: SYNCH, SYNCH, SOH, SOT, RIM SIP SIM BRR, DELLAROM ETX EOT SYNCH SYNCH!!!!

Houshmand starts walking toward her, while shouting: Dellarom what are you saying, what you are talking about. What is the matter with you?

Dellarom: SYNCH SYNCH SOH SOT NOT ACNOWLEDGED ETX EOTSYNCH SYNCH!!

Houshmand opens his arms so gently and gently says: let me embrace you my love.

Houshmand starts walking toward her: my love come to me.

Dellarom raised her hand upward toward the captain. She was taking a face as if she was really mad. At the palm of her hand there was an energy pack. People soon realized that it was a high energy pack. Dellarom was discharging the energy pack in captain's face. A surge of energy came out of her palm going through the air discharging at the captain. The captain was thrown in the air toward a wall. Captain hit the wall violently. Everybody thought that much energy must have really hurt someone. Especially after the people saw that the captain violently hit the wall too. People thought that the incident with the wall was enough to break something in captain's body. It takes a few seconds before Houshmand gets himself together and collects himself. He observed a security guard going for his gun. He presumed that, the security was going to shoot his fiancée. As the security guard was going for taking the gun out of its holster. Houshmand shouts.

Houshmand: Officer please don't shoot. She is in a state of shock. She doesn't understand what she is doing. Please don't hurt her.

Houshmand with apologizing tone: See my true love, perhaps it was insensitive of me. I know that you have gone through a lot since you have been kidnapped.

Jones was watching her and what she was saying all the time. Captain thought if he is apologetic with her, she might come around and talk with him. He was asking his fiancée to come to her senses and stop the nonsense. Every time the captain talked to her, she answered him like this.

Dellarom to Houshmand: SYNCH SYNCH SOH SOT NOT ACKNOWLEDGED ETX EOT SYNCH SYNCH.

Jones turned to Russell: Russell, I think that I can help.

Russell nods, giving Jones OK to proceed.

Russell turns to Houshmand: You have done your best so far, I think you better let Jones take over. Maybe Jones can bring her to reality and her senses.

Jones to Dellarom: SYNCH SYNCH SOH SOT JONES RTS SYNCH SYNCH!!

Dellarom: SYNCH SYNCH SOH SOT ACNOWLEDGED ETX SYNCH SYNCH!!

Captain Houshmand shouts: What is the matter Jones? Is this thing contagious?

This was funny how Jones was talking the strange language too. Everybody including Houshmand knew that since Dellarom was in the computer processing unit of the robot and Jones was expert in technical world, Jones would wrap this up rather quickly.

Russell to Houshmand: You better back down for a while. It seems that Jones has the matter well in hand.

Houshmand to Russell: yes sir I found out that already.

Jones to Russell: I think I have got this real well sir.

Russell smiles in satisfaction. Dellarom and Jones start to speak in a computer communications language called HDLC. Jones directs Dellarom to a sort of private corner. He tells her in HDLC language to sit down on a bench in the corner, thinking maybe that will calm her down further. They talk for about 10 minutes. All along Jones was not sure whether she comes around. Jones tried to make her understand that she is alright, and she is amongst friends. He thought that this might have been a very shocking experience for her. Jones told her that her fiancée loves her more than anything in the world. He asked her to remove the energy pack from her palms. She listened. With a little hesitation Dellarom started to take the energy packs from her palms. Jones took a sigh of relief as the audience sighed too. Then Jones observed that Dellarom was talking normally with him.

Dellarom: I feel that I am a victim in this situation. My so-called fiancée acted like a dim weeded idiot. I have sent help messages to him at least a hundred times. But he did not understand.

Jones: Did you expect him to know data communications language?

Dellarom: I guess this is all my fault? If He loved me he should have to do anything to save me.

Jones: do you know he traveled to another realm to find you?

Dellarom I was well aware when I was in Ultradimensions. I was inside the robot all the time.

Jones: I would take it easy for a while. We are facing a devastating war with Xinterrians and their allies the Mehjazians. These enemies hold a bad grudge. They are determined to destroy earth. From what I hear the devastation and casualties are beyond what you could imagine. Captain Houshmand is a hero amongst our fighters. Please for the sake of innocent people, try hard to not belittle him and try to see a hero of people in him first, before you see your fiancée in him.

She became serious all of a sudden. She held her head in her two hands and said after while she would do it. Dellarom started to cry.

Dellarom: do you know what it is like to spend days inside a robot? The loneliness alone could kill somebody. Every day I sit on my corner, put my head on my knees and cry. A song from my neck of the wood was playing in my head and made me cry harder.

Jones: must have been Heck of a song!

Dellarom: it basically talks about a robot called Adamac. It says that. Adamac the hearts don't have kindness. People step all over kindness. The heart of the person in love is full of pain. Let's go to god and set this arbitration to him. Adamac life is cold isn't it? Adamac, your legs and hands are rigid and dry aren't they in your chest they left are empty space in place of heart isn't it.

Jones saw an improvement in Dellarom's behavior. He took her hand and walked toward the captain.

Jones: captain as you know she has had a very hard time in the past few days. But I saw some smile here and there. She will be good in a few days. But she is still mad especially at you. I know you would be considerate with her.

Everybody in space station is smiling, when Jones take Dellarom to her fiancée. A few friends suggested to captain to go with open arms and embrace her.

An officer to Chang: Why don't we get a pool going as to who kisses who first?

Chang initiated the pool, saying: The time is running out people. Do it fast.

The bets were coming to Chang through his communicator. Chang sees the captain walking slowly toward Dellarom. Chang sends a message to everybody. The message says that only thirty seconds left for pool. No bets after that. Everybody sees that the two fiancées are walking toward each other. That made a lot of people to bet. When the couple were one foot distance. Houshmand opens his arms toward her. Everybody is watching the couple on the screen. She reached and smacked Houshmand in the face.

Dellarom furious shouted: you dumb bell! What took you so long? Were you going to let me rot in there?

This situation was much unexpected, but somehow a few people found it funny. Houshmand gently rubs his face where he was smacked.

Houshmand: My dear do you know what I have gone through? I have gonein a very strange journey and saw things that no one has seen before. I was just trying to find you. Do you think I wasn't thinking of you every second? Is this the way you pay me back? I was lost in another realm called Ultradimensions. Many things, the fear and suspense were a killer. I was searching for you all the time. But I know why you are angry. You probably are thinking why I wasn't able to save you any sooner. I also know that you sent so many messages asking for help. Sorry I don't know computers language to understand you. I apologize honey. Would you forgive me?

Somehow Dellarom begins getting her senses back. Houshmand embraces her fiancée. Dellarom then kisses the captain.

Joker: Can we celebrate and cheer this time for real? Is there another episode to this story?

Based on so many adventures between this two, joker's comments seemed very hilarious.

Russell: You know, I have had enough adventures from you two, to last me for a year.

Russell turns to lieutenant Chang: Who was the winner of the pool?

Chang whistles loud to take everybody's attention, to announce the winner.

Chang: Ladies and gentlemen. I will announce the winner in a few seconds.

An officer: Please no speeches. Can you get on with it?

Russell trying to hide his laughs with a handkerchief, thinking what a bunch! He wouldn't say or do any of the things he has seen today. He gets himself together, and begins to speak.

Russell: I really apologize but we are in a middle of situation of an eminent war. Please start.

Chang: From all of you losers of the pool, I want to congratulate Lieutenant Nikkita Ohashi as the winner.

She predicted a harsh argument between the couple, may be a fighting happens before they make peace and kiss.

The red alert on the section that included the Major's office was removed by the major. Russell turns toward the couple and says:

Russell: If you want to have a marriage ceremony here I can make the arrangement for you.

Houshmand: Thank you, Major for your generous offer but we need to discuss this between us.

Dellarom: Thanks just the same Major's but I agree with my fiancée.

Housmand runs to Russell and they talk for a few minutes. Russell orders someone to announce and call Jones and the highest senior officers to conference room ASAP. After a short time, when everyone is in conference room, Russell nods to Houshmand. Houshmand goes to the podium at the conference room.

Houshmand: As you know, I was in the Ultradimensions for a while. In there, I was told that according to some rumors that are very close to certainty, that the enemy using the teleport technology Has implanted some very dangerous bombs all across the earth. These bombs are hidden all over earth. The ruthless Meh-jazzians ordered the bombs to be planted, but the Xinterians did the actual crime. Can anybody give their opinion as to how to discover the bombs and then how to neutralize them?

Sanchez: I could use the latest, long range sensors to detect the bombs. I am not a bomb specialist perhaps on earth they can come up with a diligent cautious method to neutralize the bombs. I believe we can send the result of our long range sensors to earth.

Russell: you arrange for all technical sensor data, and I will accompany my signature to show my support.

Houshmand: Lieutenant Sanchez, add in your report that by my deduction, same technology that the Xinterrs used to miniaturize Dellarom to put her in my robot might have been used to hide the bombs on earth. The earth forces must search all over to detect these miniaturized bombs. Using normal detection methods will not reveal the bombs. For example, tell earth that we used very long range sensors to detect the bombs. I think if you accompany your research data to your report, earth will consider our statements about miniaturized bombs very seriously. Please start your research on Florida and Washington State in the United States of America. I was told that the bombs are in a pool all across a vast land. These bombs are usually in vast measure in pools in jungle areas near the body of a vast source of water. There is a vast pool in each location specified. I believe all the law enforcement forces must be used for the detection and neutralizing project. Forces like the army, National Guard, Rangers and the police etc.

In a few hours after Sanchez's report that was produced with cooperation of Ohashi, Admiral Weldman, the chief of staff for earth and the Space commission allied forces Appeared on a secure channel. Major Russell rushed to communication room as soon as he was paged to appear on link to admiral Weldman.

Admiral: your report was accurate and well done. My commendation first of all to captain Houshmand for the excellent Intel to make us search for the bombs. Lieutenant Sanchez's report was also remarkable especially that included some detailed technical information. Your teamwork efforts are commendable. Somehow the news that there are some hidden bombs on earth scattered by some character named Edenman from the Mars colonies. He now has claimed de fame as the original informer about these bombs.

Captain Houshmand interrupting the admiral: I beg your pardon admiral for interrupting, but that character is suspected for cooperation with the Meh-Jazzians. Please don't let him get away. Order to arrest this filthy dangerous man

Admiral: Do I detect a resentment captain?

Houshmand: Yes sir. This is the same traitor who arranged miniaturization of my fiancée and replacing her into my robot. We believe the same technology is used for miniaturization of the hidden bombs on earth. This traitor is smart like a rat.

Admiral: Thank you captain for the information. I will order arrest and interrogation of this man.

Admiral Weldman turned his head back to talk to one of junior officers to arrange for Edenman's arrest.

Weldman: Due to mismanagement for handling the news about the bombs caused by Edenman, there has been chaos all over the earth. Including anarchy, looting and, murder. The chaos and anarchy have caused some casualty on earth. But using our team's fine report we have detected and neutralized all of the bombs in Washington State and Florida. This neutralization was broadcasted on TV and Radio. There is a new channel set up to report the news of bombing to all people. One radio and one TV channel are associated just for this purpose. Except, every hour on the hour news, on regular channels. All radio and TV channels are scheduled for regular programming. This way we won't bore or agonize the common people with the information and onetrack minded Intel about the same subject. People can unwind with regular programming or they could listen to special channel for bomb news.Fortunately things are somewhat back to normal now.

At this time a report came for the admiral about Edenman. The report said that Edenman has managed to escape to some unknown location. The admiral looked like he was displeased with the news of escape of Edenman.

Weldman on communications link: Weldman out.

A fleet of Xinterrians, capture a small space station near the moon. The Xinterrians wanted to capture a relatively simple and easy target. This station near earth's moon is called Seema Network station, Seema is used mainly for relay to communicate with further locations in space. Seema also holds a telecommunications center. Although it does not have any military and strategic importance but it could show how confident the enemy is about capture of earth targets.

Houshmand: major, I think we are getting so close to the eminent war.

Russell: I have not received anything from earth as to when we can defend our targets. Too bad that we cannot Initiate anything ourselves otherwise with your help we could repel those Xinterrians in two minutes time.

Houshmand: You are right major. But how can you be sure that this is not a trap. Maybe the enemies just want us to be busy with this liberation of moon station. You know as well as I do, that leaving for the moon and letting Cahcashon space station defenseless might be exactly what the enemy wants us to do. While we go after liberation of a less strategically important target like moon, the enemy then can capture a very important military target like Cahcashonspace station. If you want to know honestly major, knowing the IQ of the enemy, I don't think this attack on moon space station in any of our guesses. I think Zieman khan the leader of Xinterrians hates me so much that since my sister, Nina Houshmand is the chief engineer of the moon's Seema station. Most likely this act was done mainly by Xinterrians, is most likely cooked up for me. I think Xinterrians are thinking to get some advantage from us by negotiation, now that they have my sister.

May be Houshmand was right about Xinterrians gaining some points against earth by negotiation over Nina Houshmand. But the earth allied forces did not know about two fleets of Xinterrians hiding behind the moon, while the Xinterrians intended to show a few fighter ships in front of the moon for fooling earth. The mission of these two fleets was to surprise Commander Russel and his forces. Whether Russel wants to go to moon or earth, these two fleets can always annihilate Russel. Furthermore, By Zohtarkhan the leader of Meh-Jazzians four fleets of Mehjazzians were hiding behind planet Mars as a double insurance against Russell. In the meantime earth was under attack by the enemy forces. The number of earth forces against the invasion of the enemy was extremely low and under a disadvantage. Earth needed fresh enforcement coming from Major Russell desperately. The earth allies were under another disadvantage. The earth had fewer ships and less ammunition and more at disadvantage in terms of technology. The enemy was equipped with more modern technology. However, earth forces were really trying hard to defend their home. So, earth alliance was hardly holding enemy with a lot of casualty. So far earth was successful not to let the earth itself sustain any damages. A message came from Nina Houshmand from Seema moon station. When captain Houshmand received the distress call from his sister He noticed that there is a very strange drum beat as a background noise in the communication message. Houshmand did not think much about these drumbeats at the time. However, it seemed strange to him. Houshmand went and showed the message video to Dellaram his fiancée. Dellarom had not cured from agitation and nervousness from her incarceration inside the robot. So, she started to argue with her fiancée.

Dellarom: Didn't you hear that they have arrested your sister in the Seema moon station. Don't you want to do something? Are you going to let her rot in a Xinterrian jail? You men are all alike it is hard for you to be sensitive to needs of others. Look the message says clearly hurry up and save me.

Dellarom was speaking in Persian with the Captain. Her last sentence included the word hurry which sounds like bodo. At this very minute Jones was passing the couple and trying to pretend that neither he is listening or caring about a couple arguing. Jones heard the word bodo. Then something clicked in his head 'Bodo'. Of course, Jones did not comprehend any other words. But he had heard about the strange drums in the back ground from Russell.

Jones: I beg your pardon, did you say baudot (phonetically sounds BO- DOW).

Dellarom: yes. That is what his sister told him in her message. Meaning hurry up and save me. She probably is hiding in some corner about to be captured and now it is the best time to rescue her.

Jones: I heard about the message that Nina Houshmand said "I hope you get my meaning."

Captain interrupted Jones: Dellarom I know how you are still angry at me for not rescuing you sooner. I also know that you smell rats in this message. If she is captured how did she manage to send a message asking for help?

Jones: I believe that I can answer both of you. Baudot was an old French mathematician in 20th century coming up with something like a morse code for computers. Please let me have the message and I will figure out the secrets of the drum beat. It is a long shot but still we have some hope that my Hypothesis is right.

Jones went to the lab analyzing the message. Finally, he came up with a really stunning result. Jones reported the message to Russell. He really saw that the Major was pleased with him.

Russell: Bravo you and Nina Houshmand for this heroic savior. I am indebted to both of you. You are both geeks and geniuses.

Russell debriefed Houshmand of the message.

The message:

My dear brother. I hope that you understand when I was preparing this message. Seems like you did, if you are reading it right for the first time. These Xinterrians are really stupid as you mentioned, long time ago. I told them if you give me a bottle of wine, I will send a message to my brother to hurry up and save me. The Xinterrians shortchanged me to one glass of wine but demanded that I prepare this message immediately. Off course they did not know the meaning of the drum beats. Boy they really thought they are so smart. I have some important Intel for you and Major Russell.

The enemy is hiding behind the moon and also behind the mars to surprise you and Russell. They are ready to kill both of you. Please be careful.

Love Nina.

Commander Russell: captain Houshmand, I will go to Mars, and you are expedited to moon to save your sister from your loser friends ie the

Xinterrians. Maybe you improve your relation with your fiancée now that you are going to rescue your sister.

Russell turns his head to Jones: This is twice that you saved the day for us. If I come back to the station from earth in one piece, I will really show my appreciation. Hint I know what you like to drink and where you like to go. It will be on me.

THE BATTLE SCENE NEAR MARS

ALL OF THE AVAILABLE captains and their staff getting ready to aboard their ships at the Cahcashon space station. Major Russell standing at the very front.

Russell: May I have everybody's attention please.

It was so noisy inside the ship yard. Nobody heard major's words. Lieutenant Ohashi reaches for a whistle that she had in her side pocket. She blows on the whistle to get every bodies attention. Things got quieter in the ship hold. Major Russell began to talk.

Russell: Ladies and gentlemen may I have your attention. I have seen fear and disappointment on a few people's faces. They say a brave man dies once and a coward dies a thousand times. I am aware of the difficult situation that we are all in. we are a very important part of the defense against a ruthless enemy, 2 enemies to be exact. We are helping the ground, air and space forces of earth defending our planet and loved ones. But you should know we have captain Houshmand in our side.

Houshmand interrupts: Major Russell is on your side too. And I know you are the best of the best.

Everybody gives a big hand and Hurrahs for both Captain and major. Staff starts to shout Captain and major's names. Ensigns and cadettes start to whistle. Hats, confetti, and empty cups are thrown up in the air. Seems like the morality and attitude of people are changing.

Russell: Thank you Captain Houshmand and your victory against Xinterrians. He will try to implement his tactics this time too. Hopefully like last time with the help of the captain we will have victory again. You were all debriefed by your captains some of the new tactics designed for our enemy by captain Houshmand. Try to remember your role for each maneuver as explained by your captains. Please try to remember that you will be very professional. Bad news is that the joker subroutine on Ryaneh is turned off too. After the victory you can have Joker. I have a lot to say but we only have a limited time. It is time to help earth's defense forces. I will tell you one last thing. Houshmand likes to make new strategies while we are in battle. Your ships are equipped with 2 secret frequencies. Do not reveal any information on main communications channel. Secret frequency channels are for important communications, secret frequencies usually are to be initiated by captains and second in commands.

Russell steps on the lift to go up and starts his starship. Captain Houshmand also goes to ride in Simorgh, His fighter ship that is known to be the fastest in the station's fleet. The cadettes, ensigns, and first officers etc. go to their appropriate ships.

Russell: Ensign O'harra fire up the engine. Set course to the one hundred Billion kilometers from earth.

Ensign Oharra: aren't we about one billion miles away from our target?

63

Russell: we are on the right course. The enemy has compromised our com link and Galactical Position Systems ie. The GPS. As you know Mehjazzians are notorious Hackers.

O'hara: Yes sir. Those dirty meh-jazzians. Yeah good Idea let's confuse them as if we are going straight to earth and be ambushed by the enemy. Course set. Awaiting further instructions.

Russell: Good, keep on to the course until further notice.

Commander Russell and his group one after the other went on pretending going to earth, as if they don't know about the ambush set up by the enemy behind Mars. Russell then changes course toward mars in time to surprise the enemy. Russell, before reaching the mars planet orders his staff to do specific things.

Russell: charge up the phasors. Load the rockets and photon torpedo.

Captain Houshmand group is going toward the moon to repossess the moon base and save his sister from the monsters.

Houshmand: Ryaneh, set course toward earth. At one hundred Billions kilometers away from earth, suddenly change course toward the moon.

Captain Houshmand's group leaves the station one by one.

Houshmand: Everyone in my group immediately go to roster check, after I am done. But you are to go to the main-channel after thirty second. If the enemy is monitoring our communications, which mostly is, then they won't have enough time to synch in and hack our communications secret link. Ready, on my mark, go.

Captain Sardar sahib khan of Indian forces: ensign Gian do a roster attendance forus.

Ensign Gian: This is Gian of the Shiva starship. Acknowledged.

Followed by that, other ships started to acknowledge too.

Angelito starship: This is ensign Constantino of Angelito starship acknowledged.

All of Captain Houshmand's team acknowledged, and apparently set the course toward earth. The ships headed for Mars under Major Russell, arrive in groups behind the enemy forces around Mars unexpectedly. Unlike Meh-jazians expectation, this time Russell forces were doing the sneak attack. In the surprise attack a lot of Meh-Jazzian fighter ships and some starships were annihilated. Fewer earth forces belonging to Major Russell group was destroyed. Meh-jazians still had the upper hand.

Russell: This is Major Russell. Everybody in my group go to secret one channel immediately.

Russell: Everybody knows the Houshmand strategic one tactic. The time is right for that maneuver.

All of the staff and ships in Russell group acknowledged and started the Houshmand one tactic. This tactic requires some acting. Such as making the enemy believes that a great number of earth fighters turned coward. Some starships and fighters announce that even with first wave of earth forces attack on enemy, since the number of enemy is too many for them they want to retrieve. The enemy will follow these so-called rogues to finish them off. The sanctuary for the rogues is the nearby nebula. This nebula is called alpha century nebula. Alpha century is known notoriously for its electrical discharges. This maneuver has several advantages. First advantage is that the enemy forces split up. For the starships defeating this group of enemies is easier. Second advantage is the electrical gap discharge is small enough to maneuver for a star ship. Yet it is virtually impossible for the Meh-jazzian super cruisers to fit in the gaps. This way some of the enemy's huge super cruisers following the so-called cowards will be wasted by electrical discharge at the nebula. The same thing happened. All of the enemy super cruisers that were following the so-called cowards were wasted. Russell was one of the ships pretending to be a coward. Russell was actually the leader of these so-called cowards. With bravery from Russell followed by his other comrades such as starship Yacamoto and Shih Choon. They really annihilated the enemy in the nebula.

Ensign Gian on main channel: you may call me a chuckle head but let me relive our encounter with enemy. I had two photon torpedoes targeting a Meh-jazzian starship. I told them do you really want to enslave earth? Do you want to command earth? You won't get earth. You get 6 feet of earth on your heads. I treated them with our hospitality of two photon torpedoes afterward. Then boom they blew up.

Captain Sahib to Gian with an anger shouting with commanding tone: Get off the channel. No time for being cocky. Next time I will put you in brigs.

While captain Sahib and Gian were arguing a Meh-jazzian star ship sneaked behind Shiva star ship ie captain Sahib's ship. The Mehjazzian had locked phasors on Shiva. Right then the Russian starship came to rescue and hit the meh-jazzian ship.

Ensign Theo from the Russian Podiamkin: I saved you this time Gian, but be a little more serious please for all of us.

The so-called cowards repeated the same thing 3 more times, at each wave of attach, the earthlings destroyed more and more of the Meh-jazzy-Xinterrs' forces. Each time the cowards had bigger and more of the enemy forces that would go for pursuit. A lot of the enemy forces got wasted but unfortunately there were still a lot of the enemy left.

MEANWHILE AT THE AFRICAN STARSHIP MOMBATO

ENSIGN MOTOBUTO WHILE RUNNING to the bridge: Captain Bebe, I have good news. I realized that the electrical discharges in the nebula have a stochastic behavior. I mean we can predict with some probability of certainty as to when and where the discharges will occur.

Captain Bebe: this is great way of hospitality for our Mehjazzian cruisers. Can you really predict when an electrical discharge will occur, while predicting the location of the discharges too?

Ensign Motobuto: I did not claim 100% of probability, just certain percentage.

Bebe: Bring all of your calculations, simulations and all of computers that can be useful for this project to the bridge. You sit next to ensign Abayomi at the helms. I want a success story from you two.

Abayomi: sit down next to me Motobuto. Let's make our captain proud of the both of us. Get ready in 1,000,000 kilometers we will reach the nebula. But let me lose this Mehjazzian loser that is on our tail.

While looking ahead on the screen, Motobuto: Good job Abayomi. Seems like we lost that big cruiser. But mind you just for a few minutes.

Abayomi: you want them lost now, but when we got into the nebula you want the Meh-jazzians to find us. This is what you wanted. Isn't it?

Motobuto: Yeah brother that is just what we want. Now we are about 1000 kilometers to the nebula. I say we let Meh-jazzian cruiser find us just about now. Wouldn't you say?

Abayomi: Things are busy while we are maneuvering, at the helm. Why don't you make it easier for me? Just tell me when and where you want me to be. Leave the rest to me.

Motobuto: I have got all I need. My miniature Microprocessor is ready to go.

Abayomi: Captain Bebe, I let the cruiser find us here at the mouth of the nebula. Ready for your command.

Bebe: Thank you ensign for the warning. Cooperate with Motobuto. Let me see how you two eliminate the cruiser. But till 1000 kilometer to discharge location, take a mosquito- zig zag pattern. At the discharge vicinity just mosquito pattern.

Abayomi: Acknowledged sir.

Motobuto: location 2355 mark 144 and 5 minutes from now we have 20% chance that a discharge will occur.

Abayomi: course is set. Are you calculating the best next location and time for discharge?

Motobuto: I just did that.

Abayomi: I went by the exact point at the exact moment that you specified. I am evading the phasors of the enemy. Can you find a higher probability of discharge next time?

Motobuto: yes it is coming up. The next location is a nice 35% occurrence. Most likely we will do it this time.

Abayomi: 20% is the brother of 35%. What makes you believe it is different this time. You know, I am disappointed and discouraged.

Motobuto: this is just like weather forecast on earth. 20% is good but 35% you can bet on it. The next location and time is in the pocket.

Abayomi: Captain Bebe, you heard this man. We shall see, won't we?

Motobuto: I just loaded the parameters on computer I just hope you got it Abayomi.

After zig zags and mosquito patterns, Mombatu ship evades life threatening hits from the Mehjazzian cruiser ship to the specified position and time as Motobuto had specified. In the meantime the enemy cruiser was following Mombatto like a shadow while shooting at Mombato. All of a sudden at the location specified by Motubuto an electrical discharge appeared. The discharge hit a small piece of mombato while it pulverized the mehjazzin cruiser. Everybody in mombatto ship including Bebe was jumping up for joy.

AT THE MAGELLAN STARSHIPS
ONE AND TWO

CAPTAIN HAANS OBERMYER TO captain Francois Pier: could we talk in secret frequency one.

Pier of Magellan 2: Roger. Go ahead.

Both captains go to secret frequency one,

Obermyer: This is not right that, the enemies have had too much fun at our expense. So far the enemy vessels have been at our tail shooting at us. Let's diverge and then converge at a point where we will be at the enemy flank and sort of putting them at cross fire.

Lieutenant De Fellicce from Magellan 2: I am Lieutenant De Fellicce. I have found a problem and the solution with convergence tactic. I had Help from Lorain the science officer of Magellan 2.

Obermyer: Is this the same lady who wants to get her shoe in the Fourier academy Sciences De France, and dreams about being an honorary member?

De Fellicce: I know that you have heard this from her perhaps a million times, but I think you want to hear this.

Captain Pier interrupting De Fellicce: Ober Myer, let's hear this and then we will pass judgement. I hear that she has some new tactics about flying patterns. After convergence project we will decide about her work.

Ober Myer with skepticism: Let's hear it from Lorain.

Ensign Lorain: I believe when we converge the aliens will be behind us. This way the aliens would have tactical advantage. I believe we must slow down a little bit, so the aliens catch up with us. Then all of a sudden in the vicinity of convergence we will turn on front burner engines to the max. This will put us at the tail of the enemy

Pierre: my sentiment exactly. Please upload your suggested coordinates and time and let's do it. Pierre over and out.

Obermyer: data sent. Over and out.

⋯⊷⊶⋯

AT THE MAGELLANS

PIERRRE: THIS IS BRILLIANT Lorain. This is more like a plan.

Ober Myer: That's not bad. Let's hear your plans about the flight patterns too.

Pierre: I think we want to inform commander Russell staff about this too.

Ober Myer: we just received the details of flight patterns and convergence projects in our computers. Ober Myer roger and out.

Pierre: I will have Lorrain to do the same for Russell. Over and out.

Russell: Brilliant Captain Pierre. I had my science officer study and we will pursue the matter. I will even communicate with Captain Houshmand at the moon vicinity.

The Magellans did the convergence projects up to 4 times before the slow minded aliens showed no interest to get trapped at the convergence point.

A bunch of enemy ships appeared at the convergence point. Because of high speed and maneuvers from the 2 Magellans although the enemy was behind them and Magellans were using the super shield no major damage came to Magellans. Magellan 1, 2 as planned were at the flank position of the enemy vessels. To come at the right place at the right time captain Pier and Ober Myer with the advice from Lieutenant De Felicce at the time of convergence took some precaution.

Both Magellan 1, 2 opened fire. The poor enemy vessels and the enemy were slaughtered.

AT COMMANDER RUSSELL STAR SHIP

RUSSELL: THIS IS COMMANDER Russell all pilots join me in secret frequency one for consult.

Ensign Hoshimoto: This is ensign Hoshimoto of starship Yacomoto: That darn Edenman helped the enemy track the secret frequency one. Although our ship did not receive Edenman's message. I got His message on our intelligence network. He sent something like: You poor earthlings I tracked your frequency. Don't you get my message on your frequency?

Russell: the enemy just got the frequency not the coding algorithm embedded in our communication system. I wouldn't worry for a while but they might be getting closer. Also, I have a feeling that after four times repeat, the enemy is somehow getting aware of our tricks. I suggest to start using the Houshmand Number 2 tactic. I suggest this time the socalled cowards of ours escape to behind Saturn in our solar system, instead of the nebula. It is more dangerous and shorter run. But we have to change the parameters or somehow. The enemy would be on to us, and then we will lose.

Captain Yujin of Shih Choon star ship: I rely on your judgement. And my communications engineer agrees with you about the fact that it would be a while before Edenman or Zohtar khan decode our communications codes for secret frequency one, although I was worried about the fact that the enemy has tracked our secret frequency one but not anymore.

Captain Nokomura of Yacomoto starship: I confer. Nokomura out.

Magellan group: roger and out.

The so-called coward act strategy really worked on Saturn too. As a result, almost two third of the enemy forces were annihilated by Major Russell. It was time for a head-to-head confrontation, now that the number of ships was almost equal. Time was so important for earth's defense forces, Russell had to finish the cleansing of mars from the enemy to go aid the earth's defense force.

Ober Myer at the main channel: secret channel request to captain Pierre.

Pierre: roger Ober Myer. Ensign Michelle turns to secret 1 channel right away.

Ober Myer at secret channel one: Let's extend our hospitality to the aliens. I say let's commence flight pattern Lorraine.

Lorrain: I found out that when the aliens are attacked first they escape to a predictable location. At that location they reform to attack position. I have sent you my calculations already. If we attack a whole bunch of them at point Delta. The aliens will go to point Theita on my diagram A. We need to send a probe loaded with spread domain photon torpedo. We can explode the torpedo by remote control. We will send a lot of them to Devil this way. Obviously, we won't have to be at point Theita ourselves but the probe already sent will do the job.

Ober Myer: Let's send one probe from each Magellan.

Pierre: roger, Ober Myer.

Ober Myer: Let's clean the garbage from Mars orbit. I have 5 more probes.

Pierre: Lorraine, bring your computer to work at the bridge. We and Magellan 1 have some cleaning to do. We have 5 probes each and we want your calculations for locations of the next probes.

Pierre to Obermyer: I have the same number of probes. You don't have to ask you twice. I have asked Ensign Lorrain to the bridge. She will provide the most likely positions for future probes. I will have her send you the positions of probes as we go along each maneuver. Pierre over and out.

Ober Myer: Ober Myer out.

After executing the probe project 3 more times, there was hardly any enemy ships in view.

Ober Myer: I only have one probe left. I can hardly see any enemy ships around. I want to write a very good recommendation letter for Ensign Lorrain.

Pierre: She will have my recommendation letter too. Let's make another round at our section, and we go to give a hand to Major Russell.

The Magellans annihilated many of the enemy vessels. There were no aliens in Magellans' sector left it was time to change the location. It was time to give a hand to other earth fighters. The Magellans communicate the probe project and calculations to Major Russell's staff.

Ober Myer: Ober Myer calling Commander Russell.

Russell: I am going to secret channel one acknowledge.

OberMyer: Going to secret channel one. Roger and out.

Russell: What is going on captain?

Ober Myer: We are done in our section. It is completely clean of all aliens. If you don't mind, we are about to go toward earth.

Russell: we are fine here too. But there are still too many aliens around us. We don't really need help, but if you were here, we could get done that much faster. I am about to bluff to aliens to surrender.

Pierre: I see what you mean. We will come to your sector; maybe we all go to earth in a little while to help our fighters.

—◦◦◦—

THE BATTLE AT RUSSELLS SECTOR

RUSSELL: THIS IS MAJOR Russell of space station Cahcashon. I request a parle with Xinterr-Meh-jazzian forces.

Commander Perleta of Mehjazzian forces: This is commander Perle speaking.

Russell: think it is time for you to surrender commander. You are no match for us.

Perle: You are so amusing Major Russell. I have been playing games with you, so far. I have been busy to keep you occupied so far. You don't get mister nice guy from me anymore. And I am not bluffing.

Perle had a miniature teleport device in his medium cruiser ship. Normally this kind of device is very big but Meh-jazzians had managed to steal the technology of Miniaturization from the defeated Bojnas planet. Now the Meh-jazzians have the technology to miniaturize the teleport system to teleport Bombs into the earth vessels. The meh-jazzians tried to do that to Major Russell's starship. But fortunately, Major Russell ship had about 85% shield remained. The shield was potent enough to repel the bombs sent by teleport by the Meh-jazzians.

Nothing really happened to Russell's ship. The Meh-jazzians learned that the earth forces had a super shield. This matter was reported finally to Zohtar khan the leader of Meh-Jazzians.

Zohtar: Commander Perle this is General Zohtar. Go to the secure channel I want to speak to you.

Commander Perle goes to communication room at his ship and starts to listen to his leader.

Zohtar: Edenman confirmed my idea.

Perle: what did Edenman say?

Zohtar khan: Uhh..We agreed that we should not use teleport technology to teleport bombs to earthlings. They have the super shield. Our teleported bombs won't work on them. But I have good news for you. We will defeat earth and because they are so stubborn, we will kill more than I had planned before. I will come to earth vicinity to watch the progress of the war.

Perle: over and out.

Russell to helm: I like to test Magellan 2's probe maneuver.

Engineering to Russell: sir, we have loaded 4 probes with extended domain photon torpedo. We are ready to go.

Russell to engineering: we are ready too.

Russell to helm: Ensign, Get ready for attack and escape, following by the probes, before the aliens form for counter attack.

Helm: yes sir. We are ready. But we need a science officer to do the necessary calculation and eventually spin point the best location for probe for each maneuver.

Russell: I have assigned lieutenant Omar to the bridge with his computer. He will do his part sufficiently.

Russell: all ships, go to secret channel one.

Russell on secret channel one communication link: General Broadcast. I have asked lieutenant Omar to send each of the starships the detailed plans and calculations for convergence, probe, and the so-called cowards' maneuvers. You need the best science officer on the bridge to guide the helms man. Also inform your accompanying fighter ships as to what is necessary to do on each maneuver. You should have Houshmand maneuver one and two. Maneuver 2 has not been used. Choose maneuvers one by one. We hope the slow minded enemy won't learn our maneuvers until a maneuver is performed four times on a roll, in average. That is when you go to next maneuver, and perform 4 times until you commence with the next maneuver. And so on.

Captain Bebe from star ship Mumbato: received maneuvers. Roger and out.

Captain Nakamura from Haru star ship: received plans. Acknowledged.

Captain Chien from star ship Shih choon: Received and out.

Captain Alhamid from star ship Riad: I received your plans. Roger, and out.

Captain Veladimir from starship Podiamkin: Acknowledged. Received new maneuvers, and out.

Each star ship had some maneuvers of their own, which was done to aliens. After each maneuver was successfully performed, it was passed to earth allies. Nervousness and tension were with everybody since the earth defense forces did not have the super shield. As a result, the casualty among earth starships was getting to marginal level that was determined by space commission. It was a matter of time before

Captain Houshmand group and Major Russell group could help earth defense force. The Russell group which was doomed to failure finally succeeded to clean up the 2 Army Regions of aliens from vicinity of Mars. These 2 Army Regions were originally expedited to eliminate Major Russell group, but the aliens did not succeed. In this battle commander Perle and the Xinterrian allies were wiped out and killed. It was time to go to the aid of earth defense forces that were bravely defending earth. The enemy consisted of 5 Army Regions of the most sophisticated technology and warfare in the universe. The reputation of Meh-jazzians was already scaring even the admirals. The Meh-jazzians only knew mercilessness and killing. Along with their Xinterrians allies they had owning, ruling, and slavery of humans in mind. And their plan was to leave fewer humans alive so that themselves rule and occupy earth, as a trophy for their victory. They had even planed for hunter groups to kill more humans after the victory. But unfortunately for Meh-jazzians and Xinterrian allies, things will not happen as they had planned.

CAPTAIN HOUSHMAND GROUP AROUND THE EARTH'S MOON. WILL CAPTAIN HOOSHMAND SUCCEED AND FREE THE SEEMACOMMUNICATIONS STATION?

Houshmand on secret channel 1: we are at the vicinity of 500,000 kilometers of earth.Act as if we are heading toward earth. Be ready to change course toward the moon. About 400,000 kilometers from the earth is the red zone where we would be ambushed. We have slowed down to warp 0.25. At this speed we will be at a critical point in almost 14 seconds, where we would be ambushed. On my mark, ready to accelerate toward warp and change course, heading to the hidden side of themoon. Commence.

All of the fighters accompanying Houshmand followed him toward the new course and commenced to accelerate toward warp. Off course as we know for manned missions the acceleration limit is 9gs at a time. Unfortunately for the evil, instead of surprising Captain Houshmand and the group, the Xinterrian-Mehjazzian alliances were surprised. Houshmand and other fighters were attacking the enemy from behind the line.

Houshmand on secret channel 1: Men and women on the fighter ships, give them Heck give them maximum fire at first. This way before the enemy collects themselves, we already have destroyed a lot of the enemy vessels. Use photon torpedo and rockets at maximum firing rate.

Captain Le Barron on secret channel one: I have managed to severely hit 6 enemy vessels with high speed photon torpedo arrays. And 3 enemy vessels with rockets. As you recommended, we had charged the torpedo array several seconds before course change. Gosh my hitting rate is at 60%

Houshmand: Gentlemen and ladies I only say this once. Do not waste the channel time with irrelevant information. It is a cliché, but no hot dogging no showboat and do not get over confident. Otherwise before you know it, you are hit by enemy. Try not to talk, just hit.

Le Barron: Sorry team leader. It will not happen again.

Captain Houshmand: Team listen, the enemy is regrouping. They are onto us. Attention to sub group 1 of my team "diverge from us and head toward planet mars. No time for the roster acknowledgement. The enemy would be on your tail. While keeping pattern Hornet 1, go as fast as you can. Charge-up the photon arrays, and before they start to seriously damage you, change course 180 degrees and then go for head-to-head fighting. Knowing how slow minded the enemies are, you should be successful.

Sub group 1 leader: this is Captain Rodriguez. I know all of us have been going maximum speed and acceleration. It is time to decelerate and change course by 180 degrees, on my mark turn on front burners while turning off the back engine to decelerate. Make sure to charge up the Photon array. Get set. Go.

Sub group one repeated the tactic four times. They knew from captain Houshmand that after repeating a tactic four times, it would be time to use another tactic.

Houshmand: attention sub group one, it is time as we agreed, to use Houshmand tactic two.

Sub group one captain Chander: We are going at maximum speed, escaping from the enemy, team leader. The enemy is farther from us this time. They think we are repeating the 180 degrees tactic. As the enemy fathomed, they are ready for 180 degrees tactic from us. This time, due to the fact that photon torpedo are running out we are using both phasors array and Photon torpedo array. I hope we have separated enough enemy to pursue us in this four times repeating the 180 degrees tactic. We are ready for continuing Houshmand 2 tactic. We hope that we have been a good help for Captain Houshmand group. It seems that whole Army Regions of the enemy are still too many for our moon team. Waiting for your command, Captain Rodriguez.

⎯⎯❖⎯⎯

MEANWHILE AT THE
CAHCASHON SPACE BASE

OHASHI WHILE SITTING AT a chair keeping company for Dellarom and continuing with so called girl talk: Dellarom, do you feel any better than a few days ago when the engineering team saved you out of the robot?

Dellarom while sanding her nails: Yes I am fully recovered. I can say I am myself again. You are right, I was really shocked and confused when the engineers saved me out of Ryaneh the robot. I am so sad and feel Remorse that I treated Pour Houshmand so bad.

Ohashi: I am sure you will make up for it. I know he loves you very much. But I am really puzzled from your behavior toward him. Maybe you were shocked at the moment, but do you respect him. More importantly, just between us two, do you really love him? I know he will be devastated if he finds out that you don't really love him.

Dellorom with a sigh of relief and a little remorse: Of course I love him. I have chosen Him to be my husband. I want to spend the rest of my life with him. I want to have his children.

Ohashi with a sigh of relief: You have persuaded me. I know now that you really love him as much as he loves you.

Dellarom smiles with joy and relief. Her smile is frozen when she hears Chang screaming: Deputy Dellarom, Emergency alert. Enemies coming toward us. Please proceed to the security monitor station.

Dellarom to Ohashi: I used to be a security manager on earth. Lieutenant Chang chose me as his deputy on this station. Just now, Chang called for his deputy. I think that is me. I will talk to you later.

Dellarom runs fast to the security monitoring room to meet Chang.

Dellarom while shocked shouts: OH my god. Lieutenant Chang a Army Region of the enemies are seen on long range sensors. The enemies are heading toward Cahcashon space base.

Chang: we are defenseless. We only have may be four fighters at our disposal, fighting a whole Army Region of invaders. The invaders will reach us in 20 minutes.

Chang to Ohashi: we will be invaded in 20 minutes. Do you have any recommendations?

Ohashi: I have no real recommendations. Perhaps we call Major Russell. Maybe he could expedite some help for us. I know captain Houshmand is too busy at the moon's Seema communication base.

Dellarom: lieutenants, with all due respect, my fiancée and I have discussed this very episode among ourselves. Leave that to me. I will take care of this. Just send the 4 lieutenants in charge of the 4 remaining fighters at the station. Have them meet me at the fleet hold along with four best technicians of Sanchez group to come with Sanchez at the fleet hold.

Ohashi: Seems like you have a plan. I will meet you there also. We will give you all we got.

All of the staffs that are called for, run toward the fleet hold to hear Dellarom's plan.

Dellarom at the top of a chair addressing the staff while shouting: Guys we don't have much time. Listen up. I have modified the Houshmand tactic number two, to confront the invaders. I ask senior engineer Sanchez to manage technicians to install the four fighters for what I call Dellarom tactic number one. Read the instructions as your helmsman sets the course for the confrontation.

Chang: I will not allow the precious fiancée of captain Houshmand to commit suicide. How can four fighters confront a Army Region of well-armed invaders, I don't care how good your tactic is.

Dellarom: I know I am the fiancée of captain Houshmand. But do not make an exception for me please. I am fully ready for this. Besides the enemy, based on past behavior will not take any prisoners. They will kill all of us in this space station. This time my fiancée will not leave his post while fighting the enemy, as ordered by Major Russell. Believe me I can take care of this.

Chang and the fighter ship pilots saw the confidence in Dellarom's face. Now they are more confident in Dellarom's plans.

Chang with skepticism: alright. Team leader lieutenant Dellarom, make us proud just like your fiancée. But please be careful.

Dellarom and her team leave the station in a hurry. Chang is praying for them along with Sanchez and Ohashi.

Dellarom: My team, listen up. We are half way towards the enemy. I know all of you had time to review my tactic. We only have one chance. Be very careful. On my mark ready to turn on Dellarom tactic in your ships. As you know I have personally programmed the software to enhance the Houshmand number two tactic. This way we will have a hologram that is detectable by the enemy sensors. We want to pretend that we have an army bigger than their Army Region. When you commence Dellarom pattern, it will fool even our own sensors. So, set. Turn on the pattern now. I know how to fool those numb skulls. Radio silence from now till the end of mission. My last comment is to be brave. The enemy would think we have super cruisers and several starships at our disposal. Be careful. End of transmission and out.

The enemy dazed and confused at an enemy with an army that was bigger than theirs.

Dellorom: we are at the short sensor range of the enemy. Soon we will be on the visual range. If you check your own sensors you will see that my program has even fooled our own sensors. Your sensors will show that, we have an army consists of several cruisers, a couple of super cruisers and several star ships. Not to mention several fighter ships.

All of a sudden the treacherous Edenman shouting: I want to talk to the team leader of the invading forces.

The Meh-jazzian general Purro shows up.

General Purro: Roger Edenman. What is your evaluation of this situation?

Edenman with compassion: don't get fooled, stop this charade once and for all. This is a trick. It has to be. I know that there is not even one super cruiser in whole earth's fleet. There are not even enough cruisers to defend the earth how did that many cruisers show up to defend a less strategically important location like space station?

General Purro to Edenman: acknowledged. We will proceed with the attack. Purro out.

Xinterian colonel Ripeman: What is your command, team leader?

Purro: I don't know but from what I have heard from Edenman, it must be a trick from earthlings. I am about to order to proceed with the attack.

Dellorom in an electronically enhanced voice that sounds like a man: This is Houshmand. May I talk with your team leader?

Purro: This is general Purro speaking. Are you ready to surrender? I will promise to spare your lives if you surrender.

Dellorom still with electronically enhanced voice: This is Houshmand. I have a new army at my command. If you proceed to advance even one inch from your positions, I will get mad. And believe me you don't want me mad. I will annihilate you. Ask the Xinterrians about me.

Xinterrian colonel Shaboo: Purro, listen to me. I have fought this man earlier. I am not concerned with anybody else, but Houshmand is different. I still have nightmares about him. I suggest we back off immediately. What is so important about a space station anyway?

Colonel Shaboo, did not wait for an answer from general Purro. He ordered all the fighters under his command to escape. General Purro followed him to escape. He preferred to save his own skin.

Dellarom on secret channel one: Everybody, stay on this channel. From now on we will observe radio silence. In ten minutes, when the enemies are out of our long range sensors we will commence to go back home to the space station. Over and out.

In the space station Chang, Ohashi and, Sanchez were waiting for the four heroes to come back. They were ready to welcome and celebrate specially Dellarom.

Chang while waving his index finger in the air: Enter another Houshmand. You scared us half dead. I bet your team felt the same way. But don't let me fool you. You completed an extraordinary mission. Let me tell you on behalf of everybody we appreciate all of our fighters, especially my deputy, lieutenant Dellarom.

It was time for another victory for earth and joyful celebration. But at the same time everybody was worried about earth and five Army Regions of the enemies that were killing the defender planet earth.

BACK TO SEEMA THE MOON STATION BATTLE, AND CAPTAIN HOUSHMAND

A T THE MOON STATION on secret channel one received a message from Chang and his deputy Dellarom.

Chang: captain I have some great news. I will have my deputy, Dellarom to debrief you.

Houshmand: I have received your technical data and some software called "enhancement to Houshmand Number 2 tactic i.e. Dellarom "a few minutes ago.

Dellorom: I have made your name a magic word for the enemy. An Army Region of invaders was detected on our long-range sensors. We found out that they had some unholy plans for Cahcashon space base. Four fighters including me went to intercept. But don't freak out I was ready for them. We used Dellarom tactic to fool their sensors to believe we had super cruisers, cruisers, etc. at our disposal. Edenman told the enemy by their comm system that it was all a ridiculous charade and hoax. I used my electronically enhanced voice to spell the magic word ie. Your name. I told them I was Houshmand if they come forward even one inch I will get mad. As a result, they preferred to retreat.

Houshmand: Good job deputy. I will see you later. I will transmit "Dellarom tactic" to our forces. Battle in my section has not ended yet. We are in the middle of that yet. This is Houshmand over and out.

Pierre: captain Houshmand, as discussed with Ober Myer, let's put your fiancée's tactic in good use. We thought that it can take some pressure off of our weaker locations.

Houshmand: Agreed. Also use Houshmand tactics in all sections. This way we confuse the enemy and they will shoot at some imaginary targets. We can hide ourselves in the middle of imaginary ships. Most likely, the enemy shoots at imaginary targets among a series of targets in their view.

Obermyer: Make sure that the real ship is not the middle one, in a series of targets. Naturally the enemy will target the middle of the series of targets.

Pierre: Acknowledged.

Captain Rashid from Al-Rotab starship: Acknowledged and agreed.

Freeing the moon station was not an easy task. A whole Army Region of the enemy forces, were waiting for a bloody battle. Allied forces now had a few new rabbits to pull out of their hats as the slang goes to make up for the invaders' outrageous number and more advanced forces. The enemies of earth were somewhat slow and dimwitted. After a week of bloody battle and, a lot of casualties on both sides, the enemy retreated from the earth moon and earth forces recapture Seema moon station and freed Captain Houshmand's sister from agony, disease and shackles. Captain Houshmand finally after arresting two Meh-jazzian guards frees his sister, Nina from jail. Nina was drugged by the enemy.

Houshmand orders someone to take Nina to the Hospital at the moon base for treatment. Seema, the moon base for telecommunications got back on regular schedule.

Houshmand: I want two volunteers for staying on Seema to defend the base in case of enemy attack. The rest of fighters and captains will leave for earth to help the fighters around earth. We will soon join major Russell and his team. Those who are leaving toward earth must know that the defenders of earth have sustained a heavy casualty and damage. So far earth defenders have been defensive. We want to help to change our strategy. Therefore, we have to make more effort and fight harder than before.

Captain Le Barron: Are we repeating same tactics as we have used around moon?

Houshmand: Yes but we have to use caution. May be the enemy has learned at least some of our tactics. I have communicated our experiences with the enemy too. I mentioned that some of these tactics might have been revealed by especially the treacherous Edenman to the enemies. Most likely we have to come up with new strategies.

FINAL BATTLE SCENE, EARTH VICINITY

BOTH MAJOR RUSSELL AND captain Houshmand groups arrive the earth vicinity in time to give a hand to earth fighters to defend against the outrageous numbers of invading aliens.

Houshmand to Russell: Hello major, how is everything. Are you, alright?

Russell: Good to hear from you my friend. We have tolerated some casualty other than that we are fine. Are you ready?

Houshmand: I have told my group that compare to moon Station battle, this battle at orbits of earth is much harder and we have to fight even harder. Ryaneh says hello. It wants to know what your shoe size. It wants Intel for the IQ of the both enemies together.

Russell: I have a hard time to keep a straight face I miss both you and Ryaneh. Your message about the very difficult battle ahead has been quoted to me and earth. FYI we are within 200,000 kilometer of earth we are getting ready for confronting the enemy. Over.

Houshmand: over and out.

The earth forces were using Houshmand number one tactic Ie. The coward plan so many times with success. As ordered By Admiral Charles Weldman, the chief of staff of all earth forces.It was the decision of captains but he did not recommend the Houshmand number one tactic any more.

Captain Mehran of Earth star ship Homa: the enemy is good for another couple of rounds of Houshmand tactic1. I am going for it.

Houshmand so close to earth now: Mehran don't do it. There is a Mars colony traitor in alien forces. I am talking about Edenman. Be very careful. I presume that this opportunist is the brain of, the alien invasion.

Mehran: I know what I am doing. I have the Chinese Yang starship, and Korean starship ho to go along with me. We can't be beaten.

Houshmand: You guys are making a big mistake. I will not let you do that.

Mehran: Over and out.

In 15 minutes all three ships ie. Ho, yang and, Homa were destroyed.

Captain Houshmand: I request to speak with Admiral Weldman on secure channel 2.

Weldman: Hello captain. How can I help, you.

Houshmand: Admiral, with all due respect I like our forces, not to use the Houshmand 1 tactic anymore. We know the aliens, no thanks to Edenman, have learned this particular tactic. They even know How to do counter attack for this tactic. We have just lost three starships for this Counterattack of the aliens.

Weldman: How do you specifically know involvement of Edenman?

Houshmand: Captain Nakamoora quoted me from the report from the intelligence officer of his ship. Intelligence told Nakamoora that he detected a secret message to Zohtar-khan, the Meh-jazzian leader. Edenman analyzed and revealed tactic one and the aliens counter attack for this tactic. Based on Nakamoora, both our main channel and secret channel one, have been detected and monitored by Edenman.

Weldman: I will make sure to discuss all of your concerns, in the chief of staffs, meeting today.

Houshmand: I have a new plan also for Edenman and the aliens.

Weldman: your plans are always a breeze for us. Go ahead.

Houshmand: Let's pretend that all of us are unaware of our main channel and secret channel 1 being revealed. This way all of our forces will not even implicitly talk about any confidential on these channels at all. At the right moment we can use this brilliantly.

Houshmand told the admiral all of his plan. They will talk again and do the plan the way Houshmand revealed. At this moment Houshmand and Major Russell arrive on an orbit around earth. They observed that the aliens are slaughtering earthlings, the aliens had started to bombard some of the earth's strategic locations such as, major army, navy, and air force on the surface of earth. Things were seeming gloomier at each second.

Major Russell: Captain Houshmand, it is time to engage the enemy. Let's take some load off of our allies. The aliens have started to bombard earth.

Houshmand: I already have started to shoot photon torpedo at the enemy. While the enemy is bombarding earth, their back is toward us. I am shooting sitting ducks. Most of the aliens are in my section ie. in EMENA section. The villains have changed direction toward our group and away from earth now.

Russell: By EMENA you mean the Middle East, Europe and North Africa region? I will do same in American continent.

Houshmand after a short while: seems like the earth forces are taking a breath, major. I see that earth ships are collecting themselves and their formation. I see that our earth forces have begun to attack too, instead of being a sitting duck. It seemed that the earth forces had lost their nerves before. But now, I see some improvement in our side. I have a new plan, major, I need you to keep them busy for a short while.

Captain Houshmand and Admiral Weldman had agreed on a plan. Since Edenman Had been tracing and monitoring secret channel one, Houshmand sends a private message to Admiral Weldman on secret channel one. The Idea was to let Edenman and the aliens hear something that the earth wants them to hear.

Houshmand to Weldman on secret channel one: Admiral with all due respect sir, I recommend commencing the super cruisers, star ships and cruisers that we have hidden behind earth. I want full engagement with the enemy. I will not accept no for answer for this plan. It is time we teach this aliens, some lesson not to fight with earth.

Weldman on secret channel one: Granted permission captain. As agreed you will command this mission.

Houshmand: yes sir.

Captain Houshmand and group start releasing Mines all across a certain section beyond the earth's atmosphere. This section is where the enemy would be fooled to think the earth super cruisers, and other major hardware would be hiding. Now the real challenge is to louvre the invaders to the mine fields. By order of Admiral Weldman all of the mines and bombs possible on earth even the ones from air force, ground forces, and navy was transported to the area determined by captain Houshmand by the donner cargo ship. This was almost a very dangerous gamble, but a calculated risk, that both earth's group of chiefs of armed forces and captain Houshmand had agreed upon. Heart beats of chiefs of staff is almost stopped while waiting for the outcome of this mission.

Houshmand to Donner cargo ship on secret channel 2: it is time to commence the laying bombs and mines here. Make sure that there is only one narrow escape route that I have specified. This narrow path is for our own smaller ships to go through safely.

Houshmand to his team on secret channel 2: All of the mines have been laid. It is time to louver the enemy to this area to taste our earth's hospitality. We will see if Meh-jazzin-Xinterrian alliance like our hospitality first. Then we will let them consider major genocides and enslaving on earth. On my command commence moving toward the enemy. Remember to start the Dellarom tactic that consists of phony ships that can fool any sensor, when you get back to this section behind the mine border.

Houshmand group arrives where the enemy's forces are really concentrated. In this section the invaders successfully had killed and destroyed a lot of earth defenders.

Houshmand to the Jazzia super cruiser that contained Edenman, Zohtarkhan and Ziemankhan the leaders of invasion: This is Houshmand. I have come to destroy you. Here I come. Come on and get me or else I am going to get you.

Edenman: this is another elaborate earth scheme to louver us to their cruisers that our sensors had detected. I recommend severe caution.

Zohtarkahn: let them play their game. I will expedite 2 Army Regions to destroy them. The so called cowards and their supporting menial few super cruisers, etc. Afterwards I will have Houshmand's head on a platter, then we will have earth as our own property. Boy hunting and killing is my favorite sport. We will make earth our slave planet easily.

Edenman: I hate this captain Houshmand. I want him arrested to die a slow death while kneeling in front of me.

Zohtarkhan: I will grant you this wish. This time with enough hardware we will get them and your new toy, this Houshmand character is all yours. Army Region 1, 2follow and destroy every ship that you see. But I want Houshmand alive. Don't shoot at his ship.

Houshmand to his teammates: I wonder why the aliens are not shooting at us. They are only in pursuit. In 100 kilometers we will reach the mine field.

Le Barron: our sensors show that both of Xinterrians and Meh-jazzians have charged their phasors and torpedo array. They must be up to something Bad. Maybe they will let us have it, later on all at once.

Houshmand: It is not time for getting jittery. Attention all team, I am entering the cloaked mine field. We have a dampening field and cloaking field at our disposal. Even I couldn't see the mines, if I did not have the map of the mines. Even I, wouldn't dare to go to the field. I am going at maximum speed, try not to fall behind. This way I am trying to stay safe from the enemy fire.

Edenman: we are only 100 kilometers to heavy concentration of the enemy ships. It is time to get the two Army Regions ready for the slaughter of the earth's space commission forces. They are nothing for us.

The Xinterrians and Mehjazzians didn't have any Idea that they are running into a mine field. So, they started to shoot at the imaginary earth super cruisers and cruisers first. They thought that the explosions of their vessels are coming from the earthling's vessels. The aliens know were trapped in minefields. Whether to go backward or forward the mines were ready for them. In .01 light years the two Army Regions of the invaders expedited after Houshmand, were destroyed. Houshmand saw an opportunity to repeat the mission one more time. This way he could destroy at least a couple more of Army Regions of the enemy. The issue was to louver more enemy vessels to the mines.

Houshmand to admiral Weldman on secret channel 1: Admiral the meh-jazzizns and Xinterians are doing a number on our super cruisers on section alpha. I recommend all support that you can spare for the super cruisers. I am going to shoot at invaders so that they don't have a chance to go to section alpha. But if you know what I mean maybe this backfires and more of the enemy vessels are expedited to section alpha.

Admiral Weldman: I exactly know what you mean. Don't leave the section Alpha unsupported we cannot leave our super cruisers and cruisers alone. I order you to go back to the discussed section. Stay there and fight. These are most of our heavy vessels. I will send some help for you in a little while.

Houshmand while retreating from the invader to Alpha section: Yes sir. I will stay.

Zohtarkhan: I want that Houshmand. Army Region 3, and 4follow and destroy that Houshmand and everything in section Alpha.

Poor 3rd and fourth Army Region ran into minefield very soon. Captain Houshmand and team were going at the maximum speed and acceleration and the aliens in pursuit toward the mines. They knew once the aliens pick up speed and acceleration in mine field there is no return on any direction. The captain knew the safe route through the mine field, but the invaders did not. This was the end of the four Army Regions of the invaders. Now defeating one Army Region was not an easy task but it was much easier than before. Major Russell is just debriefed by admiral Weldman of Houshmand's mission and plan. Russell upon hearing the news was ambivalent. He didn't know whether to be impressed with Houshmand's plan or feel relief or weather, to laugh at the invaders with such an expectation and attitude. He just said yes sir and out.

Captain Houshmand to Major Russell on secret channel 2: Hello major how are you doing?

Major: doing fine. May be hunting one or two enemy vessels. Not like you destroying 4 Army Regions of enemy vessels. Greeting you exalted one. How are you!

Houshmand: I answer you with a humor. Can I have your Shoes and keep it as a trophy?

Russell: I am confused. What do you really want? I know this is a joke. But to cover all the bases the answer is yes you may. Ahh I get it. You want the measure of the enemies IQ combined as a trophy. Ha Ha ha.

Admiral Weldman shouting: Stop exchanging nonsense you two. We still have a war ahead of us.

Houshamnd: yes sir. And out

Russell: Yes sir. I apologize. Russell out.

The war continues. But Edenman was really mad. He was mesmerizing, staring at the walls that seemed like a prison. Zohtarkhan and Ziemankhan also were demoralized. 4 Army Regions up the smoke, is a serious burden to carry. The agony of defeat was shadowing on their forces once the invader forces found out about the destruction of the four Army Regions. Especially the Xinterrians were really scared of captain Houshmand. All of Xinterrians and a lot of Mehjazzians saw that they are doomed for defeat. They decided to save themselves and retreated. The earth fighters now really rejuvenated while holding their heads high went in pursuit of the retreating enemy. This time the earth fighters saw a merciless genocidal enemy on the run. While the enemy was held on their toes trying to escape, the earthlings were on their tail shooting at them. This is no humor for earthlings. The earthlings did not want to be slaves and being slaughtered and become homeless. The earthlings want justice. They will not let a bunch of uncivilized savage monsters to get away with anything. Only an order by admiral Weldman stopped the fighters wanting revenge against Xinterrians or Mehjazzians.

Admiral Charles Weldman: this is a general broadcast for all earth fighters. Do not seek revenge. Please don't even pursue the enemy. Don't get used to killing while burning in hate and revenge fire. Just defend the earth. When the enemies are all gone, come back home.

The earthlings were about to make the invaders to surrender or escape to their planet.

Houshmand: Russell, can you cover for me. I am planning to arrest the leaders of the enemies and that Edenman rat.

Russell: You have my support. Go ahead.

Houshmand went on pursuit of the super Jazzia cruiser carrying the enemy leaders. He started to accelerate to warp 12, chasing after the super cruiser. When Houshmand arrived in the vicinity of the super cruiser, he started to decelerate. He saw only a few Mehjazzian fighters escorting the super cruiser. He pointed his Front decelerating engine toward the escorting fighters. As a result, the four escorting fighters were destroyed.

Houshmand Shouting: Zohtar Surrender this super cruiser or else.

Zohtar: Are you threatening me boy? I can annihilate you pip squeak, with my little finger then you might get squished like a bug.

Houshmand: we all know whose army is squished and who the pip squeak is. I am not a girl that your Xinterian friends steal and incarcerate. Edenman gave the signal to open fire on Simorgh, Houshmand's ship. Fortunately for the captain he maneuvered around the phasor of the enemy. Perhaps knowing the sneaky enemy, he guessed the time of phasors aiming at him. He also had the super shields which could mostly protect him. Houshmand fired the last 5 photons from array at the super cruiser. 10 photon torpedo of this kind that Houshmand fires, is able to destroy the super cruiser. But 5 torpedo, was effective enough. He made a big hole in the super cruiser.

Houshmand: Russell may day I need a team of space marines to help me arrest the leaders of the enemy.

Russell: right away my friend. They are on their way.

The team of marines leaded by Houshmand, engage in a hand-to-hand battle with the enemy. They arrested the leaders and the rat ie Edenman. The leaders would be taken to earth, charged with genocide and destruction. The earth court martial council will prosecute the criminals.

FINAL CHAPTER: AT THE SPACE COMMISSION

ALL OF THE FIGHTERS were invited to space commission's main building. Everybody is victorious and happy. The managing council of earth commission is present waiting in the auditorium for Admiral Weldman's speech. The fighters are talking in a hall in front of the auditorium. The audiences are loud and noisy. One common noise heard is the laughter of men and women coming out of a bloody, long, and tiresome war against two merciless villains that wanted to slaughter a lot of earthlings and enslave the survivors. The sight of villains hunting down their loved ones on earth was a nerve wrecking picture. The victory of earthlings against the invaders had already spread all over. Everywhere people were gathering together to celebrate the victory. As if it was an especial new year.

Admiral Weldman shakes hands with Major Russell and captain Houshmand in front of the door of the auditorium. The flash of cameras was blinding. Chief of security of the space commission calls all audiences to the auditorium announcing that admiral Weldman's speech is about to start.

Weldman at the podium while everybody sitting in the auditorium chairs enthusiastic to hear the speech. The admiral starts.

Admiral: thank you the council, the chiefs of staff and off course the brave men and women who defended our honor and lives for being here. I don't like long speeches. With your permission I will announce one minute silence for our fallen heroes who gave their lives for defending all of us. Everybody start your silence now.

Everybody was quiet for one whole minute. You could hear a pin drop clearly.

Admiral: As I said before I don't like long speeches. I declare the meeting adjourned. As you audiences exit the auditorium, enter the large hall for refreshments and mingling.

The officers gather in groups to converse and celebrate. Rayaneh was in joker subroutine. Its group is getting larger by the minute. It calls it the chuckle head club. The chuckle heads were mostly cadettes and ensigns form different countries. The joker was entertaining all the people with sense of humor, as promised by captain Houshmand. At this point Edenman, Zohtarkhan and, Ziemankan in chains and cuffs are brought through the hall in front of the auditorium. The villains were to be court martialed in front of the council. As the villains were passing the Joker made some loud comments.

Joker standing next to Sanchez: all of you criminals, good afternoon. As the Spanish phrase would go BUENOS TARDES. But in case of you three BUENOS RETARDES. Meaning what a good retard you are. Joker itself started to laugh. Everybody else followed the joker in laughing loud. The joker becomes more popular all of a sudden. More heads are turned toward the joker in the hall.

Ensign Utubutu while greening: Joker, why don't you entertain us more? I am having such a nice time.

Joker by using universal language translator knew the word TURN with African accent come as TAARN. He was very careful not to insult anyone. So, it came up with one of its chuckle head remarks.

Joker: You guys TAARNED the table around by shutting down an enemy cruiser at the nebula.

Gian the young humorous Indian ensign trying to outsmart the joker: You have no right to chuckle and humor with us.

Joker: I have your medicine too my friend. NAARMALLY!! I don't make these chuckle head remarks.

Everyone was familiar with the way Gian pronounced the word NORMALLY as NAARMALY. Again, the joker caused a burst of laughter amongst its audience even Gian himself. Gian was not ready to lose to joker.

Gian while trying to keep a straight face, but his lips were shifting side to side: I am going to ask captain Houshmand to dismantle you to scrap pieces!

 That caused another burst of laughter amongst the Joker fan club. Joker turns his head toward beautiful ensign June Constantino from Filipino ship Angelita.

Joker in a chuckling mode to all audiences around it: Guys keep your eyes to yourselves. Stop eyeballing the lady.

Joker to June: You guys were amazing in PILIPINO Angelito, fighting for earth.

Gian to Joker: Her country is FILIPINS you bucketful of nuts and silicone.

June: Actually we FILIPINOS pronounce our country as PILIPINES.

This time Gian feels like a jerk. So, he decides to laugh along with the audience.

A Russian ensign named Theodore who is a standup comedian arrives.

Theodore smiling: I heard a commotion and loud laughter. What is going on?

Gian while pointing at the joker: Chuckle head convention!

The joker acknowledges the presence of the comedian: AHHH solute to the infamous Theo!

Joker knew how the Russians have an accent to the phrase GOOD MORNING.

Joker: GOOD MORNINKKK! Comrade.

Theo smiling perhaps with a little laugh: It is good that I have a sense of humor. If it was anybody else from my ship, your arm socket would have ended up in that trash bin over there. Listen Joker I can out joke you anytime, anywhere.

The joker starts to do his famous laugh. It salutes Theo, and starts.

Joker: Like I am so scared. I am ready for you. So, chuckle up and get ready. Here I go. I will start first, I have invented a word in Russian language.

Theo raises one eye brow as a gesture of waiting for the Jokers word.

Joker: We all did good against the BITO...WICH Meh-Jazzians.

Theo giggling: By BITOWICH you mean something that sounds like BEACHOWICH? I know "wich" in Russian means SON OF. I know what you mean. You are calling the Meh-jazzians something that sounds like SON OF THE BEACH. I am keeping proper attitude too. I know in many countries profanity is not good.

The Joker to Theo: I think it is your turn to answer the challenge

Theo: you GUNOFF You have a word in my comedy encyclopedia.

The Joker displays a picture of Einstein putting his index finger on his forehead as if it is thinking hard, while displays this phrase: Thinking and processing......

The Joker accesses its Russian translator and finds out what Theo means.

Joker: Ahhaa! You are calling me a SON OF A GUN. I know OFF in Russian language means SON OF. Okay now you are a proud owner of a new funny word. But remember that I said the joke first. You provided the corollary word.

Ensign Kim from china knew that, the joker was invincible in comedy. But he thought to try his luck any way.

Kim: I have not heard a single comedy out of you!

Kim started to turn his head away while he throws his eye brows up and down to really state what he said firmly.

Joker: Don't worry my friend I have your medicine too. Your group shut down CHENTY of the enemy vessels.

Gian: you are chuckling with the word CHENTY. Is CHENTY part of a vessel?

Kim: This chuckle head is making fun of my accent when I am pronouncing the number TWENTY.

All of a sudden captain Houshmand shows up. He grabs robot's arm and pulls him out of the crowd around him.

Gian: Oh boy!! Now Ryaneh is in real trouble. Ryaneh, consider yourself scrapped. Your head will be a decoration on captain's wall.

Captain Houshmand: robot, there is a serious meeting with major Russell and admiral Weldman. I want you to take your time and debrief them about our journey to the Ultradimensions.

After several introductions and minutes of debriefing....

Ryaneh: So, you see I have been telling you only a fraction of our journey. As mentioned before, time is of no essence in Ultradimensions. There are infinite dimensions in Ultradimensions. We have told you only about dimension 1 so far. We got lost many times, not knowing which dimension we were in. Along the journey we met a lot of important people from past, present and, future face to face at a personal level. Important people like President George Washington or President Thomas Jefferson of the United States, or king Cyrus the great from Persia and more. At the other side of the spectra we met Chancellor Hitler, and more. It will probably take several years of our realm to prepare a report about it. But the amazing thing about the journey was that the whole experience took no time. We started to enter the singularity point at exactly 5 o'clock. When we exited the singularity the time was exactly 5 o'clock also on the same day.

Admiral Weldman, and Major Russell agreed the meeting should continue at a later time. The next time the managing council of earth should be present also.

Admiral: The meeting is adjourned.

Admiral while turning to Houshmand and his fiancée: Congratulation to both of you. I wish you a happy future. Captain, you are a lucky man!

THE END

CPSIA information can be obtained
at www.ICGtesting.com
Printed in the USA
LVHW010844090621
689685LV00004B/533